A Journey for Amelia

WILLOW CALLAWAY

A Journey for Amelia
The Reluctant Wagon Train Bride
© 2023 Willow Callaway

Cover Design by Atlantis Book Design
Editing by P. Creeden
Interior Formatting by The Illustrated Author

All rights reserved. No part of this book in part or in whole may be resold, traded, given away (unless purchased as a gift for a single individual), reproduced or transmitted in any form or by any means, electronic or mechanical, including but not limited to photocopying, recording, or by any information storage and retrieval system, without expressed permission in writing from the author.

This is a work of fiction. Names, places, characters, and incidents are either the product of the author's imagination or are used fictitiously, and any resemblance to any actual persons, living or dead, organizations, events or locales is entirely coincidental.

The unauthorized reproduction or distribution of this copyrighted work is illegal. Criminal infringement, including infringement without monetary gain, is punishable by up to 5 years in prison and a fine of $250,000.

A JOURNEY FOR AMELIA

"The West is too wild for an unwed woman. If you want to ride on my wagon train and make it to Oregon, you'll need to find yourself a husband."

THE RELUCTANT WAGON TRAIN BRIDE
Twenty brides find themselves in a compromising situation – they have to get married in order to travel to Oregon on their wagon train. Every story in the series is a clean, standalone romance. Will the bride end up falling in love with their reluctant husband? Or will they get an annulment when they reach Oregon? Each bride has a different story ~ Read all of them and don't miss out!

A grieving woman with no choice but to travel West. A cowboy on the run from his past. And the marriage of convenience that binds them.

After losing her parents, Amelia's ready to travel the Oregon Trail to reunite with her estranged brother. There's just one problem...no single women are allowed on the wagon train. So, she does what any determined woman would do when told she needs a chaperone: she finds a loophole. Paying the first acceptable man available, she forms a business arrangement with a rugged cowboy.

Everything changes for Jack when a fierce woman shows up to offer him a way out. He accepts a temporary marriage in exchange for their passage West with a hefty payment to sweeten the deal. Aiming to outrun a group of outlaws, he jumps at the opportunity to accompany Amelia on her journey. Despite his reservations, something about her spirit leaves him ready to take a chance.

Neither expected genuine affection to bloom and sorting their feelings won't come easily while on the perilous journey West. Will they be able to open their hearts in time or will secrets and suspicion take root to push them further apart?

To my family. You know who you are. Whether by blood, by love, or by friendship—I want to thank each of you for always believing in me and supporting me. I wouldn't be here without you.

one

AMELIA

Independence, Missouri 1867

"That should do ya." The bartender set the drink down with a bit too much force, Sarsaparilla sloshing over the glass rim.

"Thank you, kindly," Amelia replied, furrowing her brow as she reached out to claim the refresher and left a dime in its place.

Eyes bore into her from every direction of the saloon as she raised the cup to her lips and let the dark liquid run down her throat. The fizzy drink had a bit of a bite to it, but she didn't mind it. Not today.

It must've been a shock to those poor drunkards and gamblers to see a woman amongst them who wasn't there to entertain, but traveling by train from Boston to the little town of Independence could lead anyone to seek such a reprieve.

If only that were the end of her problems. Amelia placed the empty glass back on the bar and reached up to wipe the sweat from her brow. Trouble by way of that confounded wagon master sent fire through her veins.

After Ma and Pa had passed from fever there'd been no choice but to chase her brother out West, with just a bag full of belongings and an envelope of money to her name.

The sound of another glass hitting the bar snapped her out of her thoughts. She looked up to see a man next to her, tossing back a shot of whiskey.

Their eyes met, and a spark ran through her. He was the rugged cowboy with dark hair who had bet a pile in poker; his even demeanor despite his losses had caught her eye shortly after she'd arrived. She could tell he knew what it was like to be on the losing end of life, like her.

Without thinking, she spoke. "Tough luck at the table?"

The man looked at her, his eyes cold. "You could say that."

He didn't seem sociable, but she persisted. "I know what it's like to have the world against you."

"And what makes you think you know anything about me?" He scoffed.

Amelia shrugged. "Maybe because we're both here, drowning our sorrows."

The man didn't respond at first, but Amelia saw a flicker of something deeper in his eyes.

"This ain't no place for ladies."

A lady. The last time she considered herself one was the moment she stepped foot on that train, leaving her entire life behind. Now she was a survivor. A survivor who had less than a day to find a man to marry her if she wanted to be on that wagon train in the morning.

"I don't see any gentlemen either." Her eyes traveled over his frame, having to look up to take in the way his hair fell around his sharp jawline. He looked like trouble—the type of man her Ma had warned her about as a God-fearing woman. The advice was well and good if she were still in polite society, but there were no gentlemen lined up to wed her on a day's notice. A stranger and a ruffian would have to do.

"I have a proposition for you," she said, lowering her voice.

The man inclined an eyebrow and smirked. "What sort of proposition?"

"Nothing untoward," she said, crimson creeping over her cheeks. "A proposition that could return some of the money you lost to the cards."

"I'm listening."

Amelia leaned in closer, her voice hushed. "I need a man to marry me by morning. If you do, I'll give you back the money you lost at poker."

The man quirked an eyebrow and laughed. "You sure move quickly, Miss."

"Well," Amelia replied, rubbing the back of her neck with her palm. "I have to be on a wagon train tomorrow, but the wagon master won't let unwed women on board. I don't have the time nor the means to be particular, so I'm offering you a deal."

The man studied her for a moment before speaking. "You sure know how to sweet talk a man. I'm honored to be your pick of the lot."

His sarcasm wasn't lost on her, but she ignored it, more focused on the fact that he seemed to be considering her proposal. "We'll be wed on paper. You can do whatever you want, and so can I…as long as no one finds out it's a sham."

The man hesitated, then spoke. "Make it double what I lost."

"How much?"

"Two hundred," he said, firmly.

"That's a load of horse feathers!" she shouted, drawing more unwanted attention. Forcing herself to calm down, she closed her eyes and took a deep breath.

"Marryin' me ain't cheap," he said.

Amelia sighed. "I'll give you half upfront and half when we get to Oregon."

Her soon-to-be husband asked a lot of her, but he was the best choice considering. She opened her eyes and grimaced as a man stumbled over his chair next to them, unable to hold his liquor…not to mention another cowboy in the corner trying to grope a saloon woman's waist. At least the one she chose had a quiet calm about him.

The man in question held out his hand. "Deal."

Amelia placed her palm in his, her tense muscles relaxing a fraction. She had secured her passage west but the knot forming in her stomach refused to let her relax.

Her hand in his, Amelia battled her growing fear. Being wed to a stranger as a means to an end wasn't how

A Journey for Amelia

she had imagined her perfect life, but what choice did she have?

Her prospective husband gestured towards the door, "Let's make it official then."

Amelia hesitated. It was a life-changing decision, one that she could easily regret. Annulment or not.

They stepped out into the muggy afternoon air, the sound of wagons creaking, horse hooves stamping, and people shouting causing a stir around them. The sun blazed hot, casting its warmth over her skin.

The cowboy led her to a small church on the outskirts of town, and they were greeted by a clergyman with a nervous demeanor who seemed to know the man by her side. They held a conversation about a marriage license and arranged for the minister to provide temporary papers while waiting for the official license to be processed.

After everything was said and done, Amelia found herself face-to-face with her mysterious cowboy. It was the first sound, full look she'd got of him. The man stood over six feet tall, his shoulders were broad and strong, and his gray eyes were calm but deep. He smelled of spice and a hint of smoke from the saloon. The calluses on his hands were rough against her delicate skin as they stood holding hands before the preacher.

"Wait!" She cried, her tone high-pitched and shaking.

Her cowboy cocked a brow. "It's not too late to back out."

"No…I just," she said then paused. "I don't even know your name."

The stern man's calm exterior broke into a grin, then a deep hearty chuckle. "I have a feeling we'll never have a dull moment in our marriage."

"Indeed," she said but bit her tongue to stop herself from berating him for getting too comfortable about their marriage of convenience. They weren't alone, after all. She eyed the minister and gave him a thin, forced smile.

"Jack. Jack Doyle." His deep voice brought her eyes back to his.

"Amelia Wright," she replied softly.

"Well, I can't say I've ever wed a couple who exchanged names, instead of rings, at their wedding," the minister interrupted, his brow inclined as he glanced at Amelia's stomach.

"It's not like…I'm not—" A blush rushed over her face and to say she was mortified was an understatement.

The brief ceremony flew by, the clergyman giving his speech and having them repeat after him. Time stood still, then suddenly the moment was upon her. Jack and the minister stared at her expectantly. Swallowing against a dry throat, she spoke as loudly as she could manage, which happened to be a mere whisper.

"I do."

Amelia was married. She could barely believe it, but it was true. Moisture lined her eyes as her mind flitted to her parents. At least it wasn't a love match, so it hurt a little less not to have them there to bear witness.

As she lay down for bed that night, after parting ways with her new husband, Jack, she stared at the ceiling and pressed her fingers to her lips. They'd both said yes, and he had placed a chaste kiss on her cheek, but not before the corner of his lips brushed hers in happenstance.

Tomorrow would come soon enough, and it'd be her first day of being a wife. She knew very well that traveling the trail wouldn't be easy, but at least she'd be making progress toward finding her brother, Thomas. He'd sent letters every now and then when Ma and Pa were still alive, but they'd never truly forgiven him for leaving.

Pulling the quilt up to her chin, she sighed. If Jack didn't show up in the morning, then everything was over. She'd have to abandon her plan and face life alone. No… she shook her head. The only option was to find Thomas and his homestead. Her hope was all she had left, and she'd do anything not to fail. With thoughts of her family and a head full of worries, she drifted off into a deep sleep.

BANG. BANG. BANG.

A loud knocking woke her from slumber. Confusion blanketed her mind, foggy with sleep. Who'd be at her door so early? Amelia climbed out of bed and retrieved her shawl from atop her bag, pulling it over her sleeping attire.

Today's the day, she thought as she stepped forward and cracked the door open to peer out.

two

JACK

Jack banged his fist against the wooden door, each hit stinging a bit. He'd been married one day and already he was waiting on his wife. He sighed and removed his hat to run a hand through his disheveled hair before replacing it.

The door opened a crack, and he looked down at the slip of a woman covered in a wrap held tightly around her frame. Two wide eyes stared up at him and her hair stuck out in all directions as she tried to stifle a yawn. She was a beauty, to be sure, even first thing in the morning—with hair the color of mahogany and eyes the sort of golden brown that sparkled like a field of wheat in the sun. There'd been no ulterior motive in his heart for marrying her but looking at her would be a welcome benefit.

"Oh goodness, what time is it?" Her eyes darted around as she spoke, and she closed the door in his face only to open it again. "Give me a moment to get dressed properly."

He laughed and leaned against the wall beside her door. Amelia was a ball of nervous but determined energy. The fact that a spitfire barely taller than his shoulder would walk into his life and become his big payday was the furthest thing from what he'd expected from his stay in Independence. The trail wouldn't be easy—it never was. The lands were wild and untamed. Even though it was well traversed by now it still ate people up and spit them out.

A few minutes later, his wife exited the room with her carpetbag in tow.

"We're going to miss the wagon train. I still need to buy our supplies and speak to the company." Her hair had been tamed but her eyes were still wild.

"Calm down," he said, reaching out and taking her bag from her hands. "I already spoke to Barnes and secured our passage."

"Mr. Samuel Barnes, the wagon master?" Amelia exhaled a huge breath. "I can't believe it. You seem to know everyone in town."

"Don't get too comfortable now, you've got to pay up as soon as we arrive, or he'll give our spot away." He started down the hall and motioned for her to follow.

"Why not fetch me earlier so I could've sorted everything?"

"You were dead to the world and didn't wake to my first attempt to rouse you. I knocked for a good ten minutes."

"You're lying!"

It'd been one solid knock, but her irritated tone amused him, so he continued to tease. "I'm a man of my word."

Once outside the hotel, Jack took a deep breath of spring air. He couldn't believe how his luck had turned around. He'd been desperate to get out of town when Amelia offered him a job. She called it a marriage of convenience, but he knew better. Ain't no way marriage was convenient. A job through and through, like any other, is what it would be. But it was better than being stuck in town and out of money with outlaws looking for him. He never liked to stay in one place for too long.

When they reached the dirt road outside, he turned to her. "Let's get to the group before they leave us behind and make our marriage for nothing."

She made an unladylike noise that brought a smile to his face. He'd sure been smiling an awful lot since she showed up. He couldn't remember the last time someone amused him as much. Not since…his sister. The grin faded from his features, and he pushed the thoughts aside, unwilling to dredge up the past.

He helped Amelia mount side-saddle onto his horse, Bullet, and took the reins in his hands to walk alongside. She took an awkward posture as she gripped the pommel since his saddle wasn't fit for ladies, but it'd have to do. They made their way through town and turned up in front of Mr. Barnes's establishment. A line of wagons

A Journey for Amelia

was already set up and ready to go. Many an eye focused on him and his new bride, especially the workers for the company. He knew all too well how fast word spread in this town. Good thing they were about to leave or the whole vicinity would know in a matter of hours. He helped his new wife dismount and then turned as the wagon master approached.

Mr. Barnes made his way toward the group to address the crowd. "As I've told you all, this journey isn't for the faint of heart. The Plains are unforgiving, and unless you treat them with respect, you won't be making it to the other side. And to be honest, some of you won't."

Jack glanced at Amelia who held a straight back and a high chin. She was determined. Good. She'd need that attitude to face what lay ahead. After the wagon master ended his list of rules and Amelia paid him their dues, the two of them got settled in their wagon and placed their modest possessions next to a pile of food and supplies bought through the company. Setting off on their journey, they started riding side by side.

The wagon jostled over dips and valleys in the trodden earth, the chatter of excitement buzzed around the group as some rode, and some walked alongside their wagons stuffed to the brim with every one of their earthly possessions. One family even had an entire china cabinet strapped inside. Some people chose to ignore the concept of essentials only.

While he saw the futility of such choices, he also understood it. Family heirlooms were more than items, they were memories. And once the people you love were gone, sometimes all you had left were those memories. Glancing down at Amelia, he raised an eyebrow.

"How does it feel to be on the trail?" he asked.

"Surreal. I know there are dangers but as I look into the wild, all I see are possibilities. Freedom." Strands of her hair blew in the wind, sticking across her lips as she spoke. Her head swiveled away from his to stare at the passing scenery.

They had about thirty families with them, not including the men from Mr. Barnes's company that led the way and took up the flank. The hired hands were strong and able, but many of the men from the families looked as though they'd never touched a gun in their lives. They were weak and more prone to farming than adventure. He shook his head. If things went south, it looked like he would be picking up the pieces. But those families hadn't paid him, only Amelia had traded her coin for his services. Technically she hadn't asked for a bodyguard, only a husband, but in his mind that came with the territory. If he were to play her husband, he'd play it well. Everything he set his mind to, he was bound and determined to do well.

As evening drew near, the group stopped to eat supper and camp for the night. Seeing kids running and giggling as their parents put a pot on to boil flooded Jack's mind with his own family history. Pa used to come home late with venison slung over his shoulder and a toothy grin across his face. Of course, Ma would scold him for making their children wait to eat, but secretly she smiled bright enough to light a room. Jack's sister, Sarah, always got the best cut. She was Pa's little girl after all.

A Journey for Amelia

Sometimes he missed them, even though he didn't want to. Especially Sarah. He should've noticed she needed help sooner. The thoughts plagued his mind unbidden, and he tried to shrug it off.

"Does my new wife know how to cook?" He jumped down from the wagon seat and held a hand out to help her to the ground.

"I didn't wed to do all the work around here," Amelia snapped, marching to the back of their wagon to pull out a metal pot and a Dutch oven.

He smirked and took them from her hands and set them on the ground adjacent to the spot he chose for their firepit. In no time at all he had flames licking the air, hot and ready for cooking.

"I'm not unwilling to help, but…you can't hold me accountable if my cooking forces you to kick the bucket before day one ends," he said.

"It can't be that bad," she teased, filling the pot with water from their barrel, then opening a bag of beans to pour inside. She followed it up with a handful of dried bacon and herbs. "How difficult is it to add things and stir?"

"You'd be surprised," he said, humor tugging at the corners of his eyes. "When out on a job, we're lucky to have dried meat and a saddle to sleep on."

"Well, looks like you'll be eating like a king then." She pushed a spoon into his hand and motioned toward the pot. He took it and stirred.

As the food began to boil, a man from two wagons down stalked toward them, his hat down over his eyes and his gait heavy. He walked into their camp, disturbing the dirt with his boots, and taking no care as he stomped into their space. With a strong, swift kick he connected the sole of his foot with the side of their dinner, sending the metal pot flying to the ground with a heavy thud. Beans spilled across the earth like shed blood. Amelia gasped and fell to her knees while flailing her arms about to clean up the mess of food splashed over their supplies.

"What do you think you're doin'?" Jack's words were simple, but his voice was sharp like a knife. He'd allow no man to disturb his peace like that, especially now that he had a wife in tow, whether he knew her for one day or ten years.

"Crazy Jack, you think I wouldn't recognize you?" The rotund man with beady eyes, scraggly hair, and a tangled beard fumed as he spoke. "You owe me for what happened on my farm. And I wouldn't put it past you to have been rummaging through my wagon."

"I think you've confused me with someone else, sir," Jack said, emphasizing the last word as he scrunched his brow.

"I'd recognize that no-good, low-down mug anywhere. When you and tha-"

"I said, you've got it wrong," he interrupted his accuser, pulling the gun from his waist to point it at the man as he spoke.

The older man stuttered and spat, unable to find another word of protest as he backed out of camp. He turned to bolt, but Jack stopped him.

A Journey for Amelia

"And apologize to the lady." He nodded at his companion, still busying herself by the fire.

"M-my apologies, ma'am."

"All is well," she replied, but refused to look up at him.

"Now get going before I do something *crazy*."

The source of trouble scrambled off into the distance, finding his wagon and climbing inside to eat in hiding. Good riddance.

Jack stole a glance again, looking down to see what work Amelia busied herself with after the interruption, but he paused when his eyes met hers. She sat staring at him, her head cocked to the side and her eyes narrowed. His old life had found a way to follow him, even on the road to the West, and now he had a frustrated wife expecting answers.

Instead of saying a word, he leaned back and placed his hat over his face then crossed his arms across his chest. If you can't beat 'em, avoid 'em. That's what his Pa used to say back when Ma would burst into their barn complaining about something or another that needed to get done. The problem is that his new wife seemed to be able to gut him with a single stare, no words needed. How could he possibly respond to that? Maybe she'd let him sleep.

Or maybe not. A swift kick to his boots stole his balance, and he tumbled off the crate he sat on and onto the ground below. He groaned and slid his hat back over his head and looked up at Amelia standing over him, her lips downturned and her neck a slight shade of red.

"What in tarnation!" He stared back, his own gaze beginning to grow heated.

"You best start talkin', before I pack up without supper and leave you to sleep on the dirt." She stood with her hands on her hips and her wild hair breaking free of its braid.

In passing, he mused how beautiful she was when angry before pushing the thought away. He considered arguing about sleeping on grass being no problem but knew better, biting his tongue. "Not much story to tell, Miss."

"If you keep referring to me as 'Miss,' people are bound to get an idea about us."

"Amelia. He was nothing but a disgruntled man who found worse luck than me in cards," he said, picking himself up and dusting off his pants. "And for whatever reason seems to blame that on me."

Luckily, she dropped it, giving him a slight nod before heading back to the wagon to grab another pot of beans. But he knew better than to believe that'd be the end of it. It's not that he planned to lie, but it'd be better if she didn't know. Safer. That chapter of his life was over now. He'd gotten a chance to head out West and break free. There's no way he'd let anyone stand in the way of that. Not even old Joe McCallan from two wagons down with a grudge against him for an act long left in the past.

Their second attempt at supper was successful, leaving them with full bellies and yawning mouths. Darkness now blanketed the land and the song of the prairie at night floated in on the wings of cicadas. He helped set up their tent and then watched as Amelia crawled inside,

A Journey for Amelia

the flap closing behind her as she disappeared into their resting place. Theirs.

He paused, his heart beating heavily against his ribs. He'd never lain next to a woman that wasn't kin, let alone one he now called wife. Nothing would happen, of course. They were strictly business. But his traitorous pulse didn't seem to care about logic. He swallowed, his Adam's apple bobbing as he considered sleeping outside or even curling up uncomfortably between supplies in the wagon, but in the end, he knew what had to be done. They would be on the trail for months, there'd be no avoiding it.

Jack leaned down and drew aside the tent curtain, kicking off his boots and then bending down to step inside. He paused to tie the material closed behind him. When he turned back, he froze, his wife staring up at him with a pair of wide eyes.

three

AMELIA

Amelia and her husband lay back-to-back in a small tent somewhere along the prairie lands with no one to witness her flushed cheeks or shaking hands. Only the cicadas and the night air were their witnesses. Thankfully Jack didn't have eyes on her either or he'd be teasing her by now. Not that anyone could blame her. She was a woman of strong morals, and she'd certainly never slept next to a man before that night. Silent prayers crossed her lips as she begged the Lord not to let Jack say a word. There'd be no way she'd survive the humiliation.

The body next to her moved to readjust, his spine pressing against hers in the enclosed space. She held her breath, every nerve in her body on high alert. It would be a scandal in any sense of the word if they weren't wed.

Technically they were...for their deal. But in her heart, she didn't *feel* married. Not to mention, she barely even knew the man.

Jack had been the best choice of the crowd, but what sort of man had she formed a contract with? When he'd entered the tent, he'd stared down at her before spreading out next to her without a word then flipping over onto his side to face away.

Inhaling a big breath, she calmed her body and closed her eyes, letting her mind wander to distract her hammering heart. Their meeting and marriage had all happened as fast as a whirlwind, and now they were on the trail headed West with nothing but endless grasslands between them and their destination. Their plan was working but Amelia wasn't naive. She saw the way people whispered. The way children scattered when they saw him approach. How the other men in town would glare at him. He was the right man for the job, but something wasn't *right* about Jack.

He seemed to strike fear into most hearts, or at the very least people knew well enough to let him have his way. If only she were afraid, that'd be the least of her problems. Even worse, his presence made her nervous... shy even. The way he teased her drove her crazy but also left her speechless. She hated every moment of it. Losing control like that to a man was unacceptable and got in the way of her goals.

Starting tomorrow she'd find new restraint. She shifted her arm beneath her head, the other hand tucked under her chin. Letting her body fall into relaxation, she drifted off into sleep—the warmth radiating from her husband's body keeping her comfortable throughout the night.

The next morning came and when she woke, it was to an empty tent. She exhaled a sigh of relief and thanked God for being able to avoid an awkward situation. After dressing for the day, she exited the sleeping area to find Jack already brewing a pot of coffee.

"Good morning," she said with a firm tone, her chin raised.

"Morning, Amelia," he replied, staring at the fire without raising his eyes.

Could he be embarrassed too? No…impossible. A big, rough man like that had probably seen his share of women. Her Ma often told her that cowboys weren't gentlemen. She'd been inclined to believe it, especially with the way Jack had looked at her the day they met.

"We'll be moving soon, so you'd better prepare for the day," he said, glancing up. "We got many more like it to come."

"Mhmm," she hummed her agreement then poured herself a cup of coffee. The smell of the fresh grounds reached her nose, and the hot liquid warmed her hands through the tin cup.

Jack had started taking down their tent when Mr. Barnes arrived at their camp, his clothes worn and his hat riding low on his brow. A wiry white mustache peeked out from below the brim. It moved as he spoke. "I've got a complaint about you already, Jack."

"We handled it just fine last night," he replied to the wagon master, turning to glance over his shoulder as he folded the tent material into a neat pile.

"I warned you, don't bring trouble to my wagon train or you're out," he said, gesturing to the wilderness beyond. "I mean it, too."

Amelia clenched her teeth. She didn't know what Jack had done to deserve a warning, but she had a feeling it had something to do with his past. She stole a quick glance at Jack, but his face remained stoic.

"Maybe you should ask who kicked over whose dinner," Jack said, his voice steady. "Are we done here?"

Mr. Barnes looked at him with a stern expression. "I don't think we are."

The two men stepped out beyond the wagon to have a private conversation, leaving Amelia to cook breakfast alone. It wasn't possible to listen to their words from such a distance, but judging by their body language the conversation was tense. Barnes threw his hands up then turned back toward the wagons.

The man muttered something under his breath before walking away, his boots crunching on the prairie grass. Jack returned then finished packing up the tent, and soon they were on their way. The sun had begun to rise, casting a warm, golden light across the endless fields. The wagon train was already in motion, and the sound of creaking wheels and the heavy stomping of oxen filled the air.

Amelia glanced back at Jack's horse that followed in their wake—its reins fastened to the back of the wagon. She'd inquired yesterday why he'd brought him along, but Jack had dismissed it saying he couldn't part with his friend. Most travelers had brought oxen, but there were a few horses and mules to be seen. They required more feed but were better for hunting, so it wasn't a terrible thing in the end.

"Will your horse be okay back there?" She worried about its endurance.

"Bullet and I have been through worse. He's tough as they come, don't you worry," he said, his tone confident.

The sun beat down on them, warming their skin as a gentle wind blew across the wild grass and rippled through their clothes. As the wagon train rattled its way across the vast landscape, Amelia lost track of time as she contemplated the earlier run-in with that angry, middle-aged man. The way people whispered about Jack and how trouble seemed to follow him made her question her choice. If only she'd had more time to solve the problem.

Her thoughts broke when Jack cleared his throat. She turned her head to find his eyes fixed firmly on her. She tried to shake off the moment, but the intensity of his stare made it difficult to ignore.

Amelia focused on the scenery once again, but Jack's penetrating gaze continued to linger on her. She turned her head to face him, failing to mask her unease.

"What?" she asked, her voice betraying a hint of annoyance.

Jack's voice was low and raspy as he spoke. "You've said so little since morning. You're curious about my conversation with Barnes?"

A Journey for Amelia

Amelia's heart jerked. Caught with her thoughts on him, she flushed. She had no idea what Jack had done to warrant such attention from everyone, but the implication was clear. Trouble was brewing, and they were right in the thick of it.

"Your business is your own," she replied, her voice hushed.

Jack let out a low chuckle, his eyes shifting between the path and her. "You're a terrible liar, Amelia."

She bristled. "I don't want to get involved in any trouble," she retorted, her tone defiant.

The smirk on his face grew wider. "Too late for that," he said, his voice laced with amusement. "Barnes claimed I stole something from one of the other wagons."

Her eyes widened. "What did you steal?" she asked. *No stealing* was one of the company's firm rules.

His response was swift and assured. "I didn't steal anything. Barnes is looking for an excuse to kick me off the wagon train."

Amelia's heart sank. She'd figured from the start that his past might catch up with them, but now that it had, the reality of the situation weighed on her. What would happen to them if Jack was kicked from the wagon train? They couldn't possibly survive the journey alone.

As they continued their ride in uneasy silence, Amelia couldn't shake the nerves that fluttered through her.

She stole glances at Jack every now and then, trying to gauge his mood and read his expression, but he remained enigmatic—his face a mask of stoic determination.

"He likely won't be the last to bring us trouble," he said, breaking the silence, his voice soft and almost mournful.

Her brows shot up. "What sort of trouble?"

With a chuckle, his eyes crinkled at the corners. "All sorts. I'm not a man who seeks trouble, but it just so happens to find me."

She'd gone and married into a mess. Who knew what sort of person might show up to their camp demanding retribution for her husband's actions…or worse yet, take what they want without asking? While there was no fixing it now, she was determined to find out what he was hiding. At the very least she could prepare herself. It all gave her a headache. Amelia pinched the bridge of her nose and then rubbed her thumb against the bone where her eye met her skull to relieve some pressure.

Their first day turned into their first week then their first month, most days passing in the same way. Very little talking, just routine. Each day was long and grueling, but the group stopped for meals and a good rest, allowing everyone to regain their energy. On one particularly hot day, the usual midday atmosphere of chattering, laughing, and talking was less vibrant than usual. A stray cough here and a groan there. The mood grew heavy, and Amelia tugged at the fraying fabric of her skirt as she glanced around.

"Do you think they're unwell?" She frowned as she busied herself around the wagon, pulling out a handful of grain for Bullet and holding it up to his muzzle.

A Journey for Amelia

"There's a sickness spreading." He shook his head.

"I've cared for my share of the ill in my time, let me gather some things to help," she replied, looking to grab her health-related items that she'd stored before their journey began.

Ever since her parents had passed, she'd taken it upon herself to learn about medicine. She'd followed her childhood friend-turned-doctor around town for weeks until he'd relented and allowed her to become one of his nurses in training. Amelia studied on the job for a few months before receiving the final letter from her brother that set her on her journey out West.

Moving steadily, she tucked the items under her arm and strode past Jack toward their neighbors. His hand reached out as she passed and latched onto her with a tight grip, his fingers like an iron cage against her upper arm. Looking over her shoulder, she made a curious hum.

"Stay." He didn't wait for an answer, pulling her back to their space and guiding her to sit atop a crate he had set on the ground.

"What's the problem? I'm trying to help." She huffed and crossed her arms as she glared at him.

"I'm sure you've seen fever in your time, but if it's what I think it is…this fever ain't like most," he said as he set to work on a campfire.

"What do you mean?" she asked, her eyes fixed on him.

Jack sighed, his eyes meeting hers for a moment before he turned his attention back to the fire. "I've seen it before. It's the kind of fever that takes a man down hard and doesn't let go. It starts with one and then it…spreads."

Amelia's heart grew heavy. She'd heard of such a fever before, but she'd never seen it firsthand. Not even during her short time working in the hospital. It seemed Jack had come across it more than once in his line of work. Her heart squeezed in her chest, and she frowned.

"What can we do?" she asked, her voice trembling. Treating fever was a standard practice, but this wasn't any fever.

Jack shrugged. "There's not much we can do but wait it out. Keep them comfortable, make sure they're hydrated, but most importantly, isolate them from the rest of the group."

Amelia nodded, her mind heavy with the realization that they were stuck there in the midst of a contagion. As they sat by the fire, Jack tended to the flames, his hands moving with quick precision.

"Nothing at all to be done?"

"No. There's no fixin' cholera. It's in God's hands."

The word rang in her head and tears lined her eyes. There would be a lot of death to come, and she wasn't ready for it. Not ready for the fever or for the futility of it all. Not ready for…*cholera*.

four

JACK

Jack wiped the sweat from his brow as his wife busied herself around camp. She folded a blanket, shook it out then refolded it, moved several supply crates, and even organized their supplies by size leaving them stacked and sorted in the back of the wagon.

He'd already figured out she was the sort of woman to fidget when worried, as her body was always in motion, and her thoughts spilled out a mile a minute when she chose to speak. There was something endearing about the way she held herself. The way she cared about people. Her manner held a comfort that he'd been missing in his life for a long time.

If things were different, he might've sought her company outside work, but things weren't different. They were exactly how they were meant to be. How they'd been for years. There was a reason he lived life the way he did, jumping from job to job and living in the wild among horses and cattle. Everyone in town knew him and some even knew his past. Sooner or later, it'd catch up to him, but Amelia had offered him a way out at the right time. If nothing else, he was mighty grateful to her.

He moved to stand behind her as she folded her quilt for the third time, resting his palms against the outside of her arms. She stilled under his touch. "Fretting won't do any good."

The only time they'd touched was their nights sleeping back-to-back, and the feel of her arms beneath his grip sent the same jolt through his fingertips.

"I can't watch anyone else get taken by fever," she said, turning to face him.

Jack peered into her eyes, the wagon cover blocking the sun and casting shadows across her features. He had to admit, he felt the same way about the sickness. To see people suffer and pass was something he'd grown all too familiar with over the years. He knew the feeling of helplessness that came with it, the desperate need to do something, anything, to save them.

But he also knew that sometimes, there was nothing you could do. Life had a way of taking things away from you, no matter how hard you fought to keep them.

"I know it's hard," he said, his voice low and soothing. "We'll do everything we can. We're going to make it through this."

A Journey for Amelia

Her eyes brimmed with moisture. "It's just…I can't stand the suffering."

"I know," he repeated, pulling her into his arms. She'd seen nothing of suffering yet. If it was hard now, how would she cope when their traveling companions got sicker and more desperate? When they had to bury the dead and move on the next day.

He pushed the thought aside. She fit against him perfectly—her body warm and soft against his, and in that moment, it wasn't about a man and a woman. It was about humanity. His heart beat slowed as he rested his cheek against her brunette waves.

As two people destined to go their separate ways, he let himself get lost. He held her close. Everything he wanted always turned sour, but at that moment his selfish side prevailed.

He enjoyed the warmth of her embrace, the way her body molded to his. He wished to forget about the danger that lurked around every corner and the sickness that threatened to tear their group apart. He wanted to forget the life he'd chosen for himself, the one that always kept him on the move, never allowing himself to get too attached to anyone or anything.

But even as he held her, he knew deep down that it couldn't last. The dangers of their journey were too great, the odds too stacked against them. He couldn't afford to let his guard down, not even for a moment.

Slowly, with his brow furrowed and his lips downturned, he pulled away from her embrace. "We should go see Barnes," he said, his voice rough like gravel. "Today will be long."

Amelia wiped away a stray tear. "Right," she said, straightening up. "I'm ready."

When they arrived at the front of the wagon train, he approached Barnes and a handful of his company's men who stood around him. Their voices raised and discourse swirled through the air. Jack interrupted their conversation about minimizing fatalities as he slipped his hands into a tight fold across his chest and rocked back on his heels.

"What's the plan?" he asked.

Barnes turned to Jack, his face riddled with weariness and a look about him that said no arguments were welcome. "It's been spreading for days now, but we've got to keep going. We'll set up camp for the night but move first thing in the morning. The longer we stay in one place, the more vulnerable we become."

Jack's expression grew somber. "And the sick?"

"We have a separate wagon for them," Barnes said. "We'll keep them isolated to prevent any further spread."

"How're we looking on supplies? Will they last us?" Jack asked, glancing down the line of wagons.

Barnes sighed. "Most families ran out of water last week, so they filled their barrels in the river. One of my men knew a doctor back in Independence who once told him the fever comes from a bad water supply. I'm not sure I believe it, but the timing is suspicious."

Jack's hands tightened into fists. He knew what that meant. Rationing what little safe water left meant that

A Journey for Amelia

they'd be forced to make tough choices—like who'd get to drink and who'd go without.

"We could try to find a source of clean water," Jack suggested. "I bet we could find some if we explore a little further." Most people would rather drink river water than believe a weak theory, so actions would help more than words.

Barnes considered the proposal. "It's worth a shot," he said. "Let's make it our priority. We'll set out in the morning and see what we can find."

Jack agreed then turned back around, only to find Amelia was gone. He scanned the area, but she seemed to have vanished. His chest constricted. Had she gone off to help the sick despite his warnings? He shook his head and exhaled, starting back the way they'd come to confirm she was safe. He was responsible for her, after all.

He searched the wagon train, scanning every face, every corner, every inch of land he could see. His heart racing, Jack feared the worst. Finally, his eyes fell upon her, kneeling at the end of the train. He knew immediately where she was and what she was doing. He hesitated, unsure if he should approach, but he made his way over to her.

As he drew closer, he saw the small mound of earth, adorned with stones and bits of cloth, and he knew that someone had died. A child, he guessed, considering the size of the grave. The grim reality of life on the trail hit him like a punch in the gut. Death was a constant companion, lurking beyond the next hill or bend in the river.

Amelia didn't notice him at first, seemingly lost in her mourning. She was clutching her hands to her chest, tears streaming down her face. Jack knelt beside her, not wanting to intrude on her grief. He didn't know what to say, or how to comfort her. He had seen death before, but never like this.

They sat there in silence for what felt like hours. Amelia broke through the quiet with a whisper, her voice thick with emotion. "I wish I could've done something. Anything," she said, looking at the makeshift grave in front of her. "I want to save them all."

Jack reached out and took her hand in his own, offering what little comfort he could. He didn't say anything at first, but eventually, he spoke.

"There's nothing you could've done," he said, looking into her eyes filled with sorrow. "It's the trail. It's hard on everyone."

Amelia looked at him, tears still streaming down her face. "I know," she said. "But it's hard to accept."

Jack didn't say anything, but he squeezed her hand, offering what little comfort he could. They sat there for a while longer, lost in their thoughts and their grief. Finally, they stood, neither one of them wanting to linger any longer. As they made their way back to their wagon, Jack felt a sense of unease. Death was a constant on the trail, and he knew that there would be more graves before they reached the end of their journey.

By the time they got back to their camp, the sun had sunk low on the horizon. Jack and Amelia were both exhausted, but neither one of them was ready to consider

A Journey for Amelia

going to bed yet. They built a small fire to ward away some of the evening chill. As they sat beside it, talking about what had happened that day, a figure emerged from the shadows of the adjacent wagon and approached them hesitantly.

Jack tensed, unsure of the person's intentions. He motioned for Amelia to stay where she was while he stood up to face the figure. As he did so, a pale young woman stepped into the firelight.

He hesitated before inviting her close enough to talk while keeping their distance. She came forward and sat across from them by the campfire.

Jack and Amelia exchanged a glance before Amelia spoke first. "Can we help you?" she asked gently.

The woman studied them before speaking. "I'm Mary," she said. "My son he…died of fever yesterday." Her voice cracked as tears trickled down her cheeks, followed by a soft sobbing noise. "I don't mean to be a bother, but I had to get some air away from my husband. I saw you two today, at my son's grave."

"I'm sorry for your loss. You're welcome here as long as you need," he replied.

He assured her she could stay for a while after she shared that she and her husband's combined grief had been too much for her to bear. The man had gotten sick after her son, and she needed a walk to clear her head after he fell asleep.

Amelia and Mary began to chat and soon found that their experiences were similar. They shared many common thoughts on both love and loss. As they talked, Jack observed the women.

Amelia listened to the woman's story, sympathizing, and empathizing with her in a way that he didn't understand. His heart swelled with admiration for this woman who'd been through so much, yet still found the courage to be kind. He made sure not to stare too long though, reminding himself firmly not to get attached. Even if he did give himself permission to let his feelings grow, there was no way she would ever accept a man like him.

The conversation moved away from the sorrowful, towards more lighthearted stories of past adventures with family and friends. The women shared both mournful and nostalgic words. Enjoying the cool breeze, Jack moved to set up their tent as the two talked, his mind drifting inward as he stepped away.

The sun disappeared and Mary finally bade them farewell, disappearing into the night. Jack and his wife remained awake a while longer, basking in the warmth of the fire and each other's company before retiring for the evening.

"You were awfully silent," she said as they settled in beneath the quilted blanket.

Amelia had spoken to Mary about her family, and the memories stirring within him swirled like a building storm. His history was marred by painful events, and he'd been trying to forget it ever since. He knew he had to tell Amelia something, but he wasn't sure how much he should reveal.

A Journey for Amelia

"I've been thinking about how there are parts of my past I'm not proud of. Things I wish I could take back," he said, breaking the silence.

Amelia turned to face him, worry lines etched upon her forehead. "What do you mean?"

Jack took a deep breath, searching for the right words. "I've done things I regret. And it's not just about me, it's about the people I've hurt along the way."

Amelia's expression softened. "We all have things we're not proud of, Jack. It doesn't have to define us."

He appreciated her understanding. "I know, but sometimes it feels like it's all I am. Like I'm still that person, even though I've left that life behind."

Amelia reached out and took his hand, squeezing it. "You're not that person anymore, Jack. You're here with me, on a journey West to begin anew. That's what matters."

Jack smiled. Her words were kind even if misguided. There was no way for her to know who he was, not yet anyway. He couldn't tell Amelia everything about his past, but for now, her words were enough to keep him going.

five

AMELIA

Sickness swirled through the air, the grief heavy upon her heart as she ran. The slap of her boots against the broken pieces of earth, once split by wagon wheels, echoed across the plains. Darkness covered the land in a blanket of creeping fog.

"Jack!" she cried out for him to no avail. No sign of him in the wagon or in their tent.

A chill raced over her skin and stray rain droplets splashed over her shoulders as she moved from wagon to wagon. Each one empty. Deserted. Where had everyone gone?

She climbed up to peek into another. "Mary? Are you there?"

All that lay in the space once occupied by her new friend's family were a few disheveled blankets and their scattered, broken belongings. A cold sweat covered her from head to toe, and she cried out as she tore herself away.

"Someone? Anyone?" She ran faster now, making her way to the front of the wagon train—at least she figured it was the front as she peered through the fog that clung to her skin like clammy fingers.

"They're gone, Miss Wright." A deep, cold voice spoke from within the inky darkness.

"W-what do you mean?" She stopped running, pausing to wrap her arms around her body. No, that couldn't be right. They couldn't all be gone.

"Passed on to a better place." The disembodied voice took on corporeal form as the wagon master stepped out of the fog and stood before her.

"You're wrong!" Amelia shouted, backing away. Her foot caught on a mound of dirt, and she stumbled, nearly tumbling to the ground before catching herself.

Standing on shaky legs, she noticed the dirt was piled with stones and two sticks forming a cross, tied together with strips of cloth. A grave. She stepped over it as her stomach lurched, only to come into range of another. Then another. The ground around her was littered with buried bodies that hadn't been there minutes ago.

"Amelia." Another voice called out her name. It wasn't Mr. Barnes this time...it sounded like—no, it couldn't be. Mother?

"Ma. Where are you?" She stepped between graves, searching for the owner of the voice.

"Amelia."

"Ma. I want to help you," she said as she raced past the wagons, into the darkness.

"Amelia."

"Amelia!" The voice wasn't her Ma at all anymore, it sounded masculine. Familiar.

She woke, bolting upright as perspiration beaded along her forehead. She gasped for air in heaving breaths. Two strong arms wrapped around her. Clinging to the strong frame, she looked up into Jack's eyes.

"You're safe. It's okay, you were dreaming." He soothed her, caressing her hair with his open palm as he rubbed her back with the other hand.

"The nightmare…it felt so real," she said, choking back a sob. "You're alive."

"I'm not going anywhere."

"They were all gone." Her heart still beat traitorously, but Jack's warm presence began to calm her nerves.

"It wasn't real."

Perhaps the dream wasn't, but the cholera was. She frowned. The more awake she became the more she realized the intimacy of their embrace. She backed out of his arms and smoothed her hands through her hair.

Unable to meet his gaze, she glanced down at the blankets. "Thank you for waking me."

They barely knew each other, but there was something about the way her husband carried himself that intrigued her. No matter how much trouble stuck to him, he somehow made her feel safe. If life were different, she'd have let him court her. But it wasn't. And she wouldn't.

A Journey for Amelia

After Amelia lost her parents, her view of the world had shifted. People close to her became more precious but anyone else finding their way into that inner circle proved more difficult than ever. She loved fiercely but she also mourned fiercely. If she didn't love, then she wouldn't have to hurt. The world they lived in was cruel. Sickness didn't discriminate, and death welcomed all with open arms. Young or old. Rich or poor. No matter how unfair.

"Let's get moving," Jack said, interrupting her thoughts.

"Shouldn't we let the sick rest?" She waited for him to stand and turn his back, as he did for her every morning, and she dressed quickly as they spoke.

"We need to find clean water." He cleared his throat. "And today's the day I teach you how to hunt."

"Didn't we pack rations?" She followed him outside to help prepare breakfast.

"We did, but wait and see," he said as he lit their campfire. "When people grow desperate, there'll be fights and stolen goods. This is only the beginning."

All that tragedy they'd already faced, and it had just started? Her face paled and she wondered, not for the first time, if she'd made a mistake traveling West.

They sat by the fire, savoring every bite of their biscuits and sipping on the strong, bitter coffee that he'd brewed. She admired the way the morning sun illuminated Jack's rugged features as he ate, a Winchester rifle resting by his side.

"You ready for today's hunt?" he asked, flashing a grin.

She smiled in return. Jack seemed like a skilled hunter, and she was determined to learn as much as she could from him.

He got up, picked up his rifle, and handed Amelia her own gun. "First of all," he said, "let me show you how to load that thing properly."

Proceeding to teach her how to handle and care for it, he ensured that she understood. She listened, hanging on to his every word.

Afterward, Jack led the way as they broke off from the wagon train, navigating the terrain with ease. As they walked, Amelia's eyes darted around, scanning the landscape for any sign of prey.

"Jack, how will we find fresh water?" she asked.

He paused, scanning the horizon before responding. "I'm keeping an eye out for it. And with luck, we'll find some game while we're at it."

They trekked a good way in silence. As the two of them walked, Amelia looked from one side to another, scanning the landscape. Her body tensed, and her heart plummeted, knowing that their search wouldn't be easy.

"I don't see any wildlife or water," she said, her voice strained. "Just miles of clouds and rolling hills."

Jack stopped in his tracks to stare at the sky, his broad shoulders facing the horizon. After a moment, he turned to her. "We'll find a way. If the weather doesn't push us back first."

As they continued, she couldn't help but be drawn to the man by her side. He was kind and caring, but she knew she had to stay focused.

"Amelia," he whispered, "Look. Over there."

Her thoughts were interrupted and a rustle in a nearby bush drew her full attention. She peeked around him and saw two small rabbits hiding there.

He motioned for her to follow his lead.

"Okay," he said, "line up the sight and aim." He guided her arm until it was steady and pointed toward the rabbits before stepping back.

Amelia held her breath in anticipation, ready to try. But as she was about to pull the trigger, one of the rabbits took off and scared the other away, ruining her chance at a clean shot. She let out a small sigh and lowered the weapon.

Jack chuckled, patting her shoulder. "Don't worry. You'll get another chance," he reassured her. "Also, don't hold your breath next time. Shoot as you exhale."

He took off after their prey's trail and she followed. As they stalked through the grass, Amelia gained a sense of growing pride. Even though she'd missed the chance to shoot, she was grateful for the opportunity to learn. To be a part of an adventure.

However, their triumph was short-lived as they heard the booming sound of thunder. The sky darkened, and raindrops began to splash around them. They'd been too focused to notice that the storm arrived quicker than expected.

Amelia's gut twisted as she realized the danger they were in. It was no secret that storms on the plains could be violent and unpredictable. She caught up with Jack as he turned to lead them, trudging through the rain-soaked terrain. Though she put on a brave face, uncertainty about their journey lingered. A journey that had led to thirst, sickness, and even death.

"At least we can gather the rain when we return." She tried to look on the bright side, ignoring the throbbing of her head.

"It's a good start." Jack engaged with her but the look on his face was distant, detached as though deep in thought.

"I've never seen a storm move like that," she said, staring up at the angry black clouds rolling in around them.

"We need to move faster." He grabbed hold of her arm and rushed her as he sped up his pace.

Taking big steps to keep up, she pushed forward, glancing over her shoulder to track the approaching storm. The clouds had become twisted and ominous, wrapping around each other in a dark embrace.

"Jack!"

"I know, I see it," he said, his voice tight as the walk turned into a jog.

Panic pierced straight through her like an arrow as the clouds formed a funnel shape and touched down not far from them. It happened so fast that it took her brain a moment to process. The way Jack's grip on her hand tightened it was clear he saw it too.

Then they were running. All burning legs and blurred vision. Every possession was left strewn upon the ground like fallen soldiers. The wind rushed past, whipping her hair into her face as she tried to scream, but her voice got swallowed whole by the raging tempest. Rainwater flew

A Journey for Amelia

from every direction, no longer falling straight down, as it stung their skin with unnatural force.

"We won't make it!" She yelled but no one could hear.

Despite the noise, at least they seemed to understand each other. Jack yanked at her arm, pulling her to the ground face-first into wet prairie grass. They rolled down a slight incline, their bodies settling within a dip in the hills of the plains. When the inertia stopped and they lay still, he covered her body with his own. She gasped as his weight pushed her into the sod, his wide frame covering hers completely as they lay there waiting for the inevitable. For the storm to pass…to hopefully spare them.

Heart slamming against her chest, she stared into his eyes. She expected the cold and collected gray they usually held, but the fear in them mirrored her own. At that moment, they shared something beyond a physical sensation. They shared what could be the final moments of their lives.

Don't cry, don't cry, she repeated to herself. She refused to give up. To let go. *Please send your angels to protect us, Lord*, she prayed.

As the tornado moved over them, Jack broke eye contact and pulled her closer—his arms wrapping around her head to protect her from harm. His cheek pressed to hers as they clung to each other. A wind unlike any she'd ever experienced tore at their bodies, pushing and pulling like the clawed hands of demons trying to drag them into purgatory.

Debris flew around them, branches colliding with their bodies. The storm raged, and she was sure every second would be her last. But then, the unexpected happened. The storm passed as quickly as it had arrived, moving beyond them. Mother nature seemed cruel, passing over the land with no regard for the destruction left in its wake.

Amelia slowly opened her eyes and released her tight grip on Jack's shirt. He rolled off her, and they lay there in silence for a few minutes—the only sound coming from their deep breaths and beating hearts.

She tried to sit, her body heavy with the weight of drained energy. But rather than cowering in fear, a spark of hope grew inside her chest. The same hope that kept her sane in the face of death—the hope that brought them to this place and time and allowed them to live.

Jack rose to his knees, breathing heavily as he looked around. He stood first, then reached down to help Amelia get up from the ground and back to her feet. Her legs shook beneath her, but she managed to stand strong beside him.

Observing the aftermath, she realized how far they'd run. Debris littered the plains and the sky had yet to regain its full brightness.

"Where are we?" Amelia asked, wishing she had a compass in hand. Running from a twister and ending up at the bottom of a hill would get anyone turned around.

"Lost." His voice was firm again. It looked as though he'd collected himself after all.

She swallowed and cleared her throat, gazing up at the sky as she sighed.

Lost.

six

AMELIA

The ache in her legs slowed her down more than she'd hoped. Amelia followed Jack over the plains, traveling up and down the rolling hills until the sun threatened to fade beneath the horizon. Shades of pink and orange decorated the skyline, and the air grew colder as a crisp breeze flitted through the prairie grass, causing it to twist and bend around their calves.

"We should've found them by now," she said, clenching folds of fabric as she hiked up her dress to stride more surely.

"There are variables to consider." He spoke without turning, his pace still as brisk as when they had started. "We're fortunate the storm was small when it hit us, who knows how large it'd grown by the time it hit them."

Did that man never tire? She groaned and then raced to catch up, settling into a rhythm alongside him. For every step he took, her smaller gait forced her to take at least two to keep up.

"What if we'd stayed put? They'd have searched for us." Her question hung in the air as they walked.

"If there'd been no storm, sure. But that tornado changed things." He shook his head firmly.

"We'd be by the fire right now eating a hot meal." The blood in her body heated, and her eyes bore into him. She knew it wasn't his fault, but her mood was frayed.

"Had we waited, we'd have been caught without shelter or any sort of protection against predators come nightfall," he replied, his tone stiff and matter-of-fact.

"You're a cowboy; you've spent many nights out in the open." Amelia knew her words were harsh, but the day drained her not only of strength but also of manners.

"A cowboy has his horse, the cattle, his fellow cowboys. If danger approaches while asleep, you'll sure as well know it with that many on hand."

She considered his words as she stumbled over a large, cracked tree limb. Life as a cowboy must've been difficult for him day in and day out. What drove him to embrace such a way in the past? A frown tugged at the corners of her mouth, and she sighed. "We have the two of us."

"No horses, no guns. I've no need to guess how that'd turn out." He reached out a hand to steady her after she stumbled again.

"But what if they had come?" Her heart constricted at the thought of the wagon train looking for them to no avail.

"You may not've noticed, but we've circled a few times today." Jack tilted his head to the right and then left. "We've covered several miles in every direction. If they were close by, we'd have found them."

"Are you saying they left without us?" Her voice pitched higher than usual as worst-case scenarios ran through her head.

"I'm saying when you have a tornado bearing down on you, you'll think about the many before you think about the few."

"We're going to die out here," she said, a hand clutched to her chest.

"I won't let that happen."

"You can't promise that."

"I've seen debris from the camp scattered around. While the winds could've carried it anywhere, it's more concentrated in that direction," he said, indicating a path behind them.

"Then why are we headed this way instead?"

"We'll camp for the night when we reach that rock formation," he said, pointing toward a looming butte in the distance, "then we'll pick up the trail in the morning."

"If we rest when they rest, we'll never catch them!" she shouted, unable to keep her feelings bottled up any longer.

"Once out of the path of the storm, they'd need to do repairs. We'll find them." His voice took on a soothing tone. "It's better to rest and use our full energy to search instead of getting caught in the open at night."

Amelia's heartbeat slowed as she took a deep breath and tried to release the tension that'd built up in her muscles, her body easing a fraction with Jack's words. She had to trust him. It was the only thing keeping them alive in such a dire situation. The sun slipped lower in the sky as they trudged forward, pushing ever closer to the rock formation. The aftermath of the tornado had left nothing but devastation in its wake. Debris, mangled branches, and an uprooted tree littered the ground, reminding her of the sheer damage that had been done. She prayed that the wagon train was safe.

As they walked, Amelia's gaze rose to the sky. The clouds had darkened as if warning of danger ahead. Her skin prickled, the wind picking up to send a chill across her body. Not again. Please, no more storms. Jack must've noticed her discomfort because he placed a gentle hand on her shoulder. They walked on in silence, each lost in their own thoughts.

Once they reached their destination, they found a decent spot to rest beneath an overhanging ledge. A pang of unease hit her as they settled in for the night. The darkness was oppressive, swallowing them whole, and the howling wind made her skin crawl. But having her husband beside her made her a bit braver. Even if he was her husband only in name. They huddled together, beside the fire Jack had built, as the night grew cold.

A Journey for Amelia

"Thank you," she said in a soft voice. Once the adrenaline of the day began to wear off, she realized how much Jack had done to keep her safe.

"No need to thank me. I'd have done it for anyone."

He'd have done the same for any person. That shouldn't bother her as much as it did, yet her forehead crinkled, and her chest grew tight. Ever since she'd lost Ma and Pa, she hadn't felt special. Protected. Not until today.

Folding her arms around her middle, she recalled what it was like to have him cover her and wrap his arms around her head in a protective embrace. She didn't want a man with secrets. A gambling man. A cowboy. He was everything that she didn't want, and yet…he brought out a burning curiosity within her.

"Why did you decide to become a cowboy?" she asked, acutely aware of how their arms and legs pressed against each other as they sat side by side, backs against the sandstone.

"If you can't fight your demons, there's no better way to run from them than to ride with cattle," he said as the firelight illuminated his face. "There's something about the plains that cures a man of his woes."

"How so?"

"When I'm beneath miles of painted sky, the land is just an anchor. My life…my past is just a dream." He crossed his legs and closed his eyes as he spoke.

"Sometimes I wish I could forget too. But our pasts, no matter how painful, are memories. With those we'll never truly be alone," she said, images of her family flooding her mind.

He chuckled. "Funny, I used to say something similar. But in our lowest moments, solitude might be our only companion. I, for one, find it peaceful. It's when I hear God most clearly."

"Don't you ever get lonely?" Amelia placed a hand on his bicep, to let him know he wasn't alone, but his muscles tensed beneath her touch.

He paused, hummed a deep sound then replied. "Sometimes."

"What are you running from?" The question lingered on her tongue as she waited. She'd been wanting to ask it for a long time.

That seemed to strike a nerve as he jerked his head to stare at her before glancing back out past the fire. "I've done some things I can't take back. I…used to run with a bad crowd. I thought we acted in the name of justice, but now I know better."

Pushing for answers tempted her but she refrained. She didn't know how to respond or how to help….so she let it go. The way he spoke frightened her at times. Answers still evaded her, and for all she knew he could be a criminal. Yet somehow, she doubted it. Perhaps it was his kindness or his gentle demeanor during their worst moments that convinced her.

Despite her exhaustion, slumber refused to embrace her. Every crackle of twigs caused her to quake, and the darkness closed in on them from all sides. She couldn't shake the feeling that they were being watched. But when she couldn't bear it any longer, sleep came.

A Journey for Amelia

The night grew long and restless. Amelia tossed and turned, her vivid nightmares torturing her still. Each time she woke, Jack was there, his steady breathing a reassuring presence. For the second time that day, she wondered if they would make it back alive.

Dawn broke, and she stirred as the world stood still and quiet as if holding its breath. Jack busied himself between tending the fire and scanning the horizon. Amelia sat up, rubbing her eyes. Stiff and sore from sleeping among rocks, she stretched and groaned. Exhaustion lingered within her, but the prospect of finding their way back to safety gave her renewed energy.

Jack offered a hand to help her up. "Let's move."

As the sun rose over the barren landscape, they began their journey. Moving on from camp didn't take long since all they had was a campfire. A sense of unease hung over them as they trekked over the wide-open plains, and Amelia swallowed, her throat dry. They'd been separated from the wagon train for a full day, and every passing moment brought them closer to dehydration.

With no food or water left, they set out towards the west, scanning the horizon for any sign of life. The unforgiving terrain wore her down with each passing mile. Her thirst grew unbearable, and the sun beat down with unrelenting fury. But she pressed on, driven by the hope that they might soon be reunited with their fellow travelers.

As they crested a rise, that glimmer of hope appeared on the horizon. A figure, mounted on a horse, was making its way toward them. For a moment, she wished to rejoice. She raised her hand to wave, but her unease grew as the figure loomed ever closer. She had no way of knowing if the person was a friend or foe. Jack grabbed her arm and dragged her into cover behind a bush, as there was nowhere to run. They were out in the open, vulnerable, and defenseless.

"Who is it?" she asked, trying to peek around the foliage.

"Quiet," he whispered, placing a hand over her mouth to silence her.

Whoever it was, it was too late to hide from them. The pounding hooves grew closer, the rhythm aligning with her heart pounding within her chest. Louder and louder, it grew. She couldn't tell if it was the rider or her pulse heavy in her own ears. Squeezing her eyes shut, she prayed.

Suddenly, the rider was upon them. In a flurry of dirt and wind, he slid to a stop. She squinted to look upon their fate. Stifling a sob, she stared upon a native covered from head to toe in handcrafted leather, beads, and feathers. His horse was piled with supplies and the rider dismounted in a swift, fluid motion.

Jack pushed her behind him, his body blocking her despite their lack of defenses. She could see over his shoulder as the native knelt and reached for something strapped to his belt.

Tears broke free, streaming down her face. They lived through the storm just to meet their fate at the end of a native's blade.

seven

JACK

As Jack stared blankly ahead, he wondered why. Why had he pushed his body in front of Amelia? Perhaps because she was a woman, or maybe because legally he was her husband. But he knew there was more to it. It wasn't the first time. He recalled the way their eyes had met during the storm. She hadn't shed a tear. Her face had been stoic even though he knew she'd been terrified.

The native's long, toned arm reached toward his belt. Jack's body tensed as he waited for the attack. If fortune favored him, he could catch the blow and turn the tide of the fight.

But as the man's arm moved, Jack looked up at his face. The native wore a necklace of familiar trinkets. Recognition sparked and everything changed. The native wasn't an enemy warrior. He was Running Deer, a trader their people had regularly bartered with on trips over the trail. He'd met him in Independence several times when he and his father had arrived to trade their furs and hides.

Tension fled his body, and he relaxed his stance.

"Old friend. What're you doing out here?" the trader asked, amusement playing upon his face. "I met with your people several hills over, to the west."

It had to be them. They were a few miles away from being reunited with the wagon train. Wiping sweat from his brow with the back of his hand, he flashed a bright smile.

"Praise God," Amelia exclaimed, squeezing his arm from her place behind him.

"Indeed," he said, placing a reassuring pat over her hand.

Their weary faces must've shown because Running Deer offered them a drink from an animal hide flask and some pieces of dried meat. As they ate, he shared his knowledge of the area and advised them on the best path to take to reach the wagon train. Jack thanked him and shook his hand firmly before bidding him farewell.

"Let's get moving again before the group continues their travels," Jack said, leading his companion in the direction they'd been pointed toward. "We're almost there."

"Do you think they looked for us?" she asked.

"They likely figured us dead, lost to the storm." Even as he said it, the message hit him in the gut. He couldn't remember the last time he'd been close to someone who would look for him.

Over time he'd convinced himself that he didn't mind being alone. Yet for some reason, ever since Amelia had shown up, he'd felt…different. Their relationship hadn't progressed so far as to call it anything it wasn't, but having someone to think of him and to think of in return was more than he expected. He'd mark it under another reason he protected her that day.

He put that thought away, not liking to dwell on such feelings. As they crested the hill, what remained of the wagon train dotted the valley below and he exhaled some of the tension from his body. A frown crossed his features as he counted how many wagons were left after the storm. Most were quite worse for wear.

"Jack, they're gone…the storm took them." Her hushed voice sounded tight as she peered around him.

"We won't know until we get down there." His words were brief, but his heart ached.

There was no point worrying over what couldn't be changed. Large strides carried him to the destination as he paused along the way to make sure his companion still followed. Their steps lagged at a distance until the group stopped to rest, allowing them to catch up on foot. When they reached camp, a familiar face greeted them.

Mary ran through the small crowd, shouting their names as she waved her arms through the air.

"Thank God you're alive. I thought we'd lost you to the storm." She began to sob, and Amelia soon joined her. The two women hugged as they cried, forgetting any worry of illness.

They hadn't known Mary for more than a day or two, so it perplexed him as to why the two were bonded enough to weep together, even if they'd just survived a disastrous event. The ways of women continued to perplex him, but he nodded and excused himself to go find Barnes.

Reality set in as he made his way through the camp. Twisted metal and splintered wood poked out from the wagon frames. They were once packed to the brim but now looked as if they could barely make the journey ahead.

As he searched for Barnes, he wondered how the man had managed to keep the group together in the aftermath of the storm. He found him sitting alone near one of the wagons, his face haggard and downcast. Barnes raised his head as he approached with heavy steps.

"You made it out alive," the man exclaimed, his voice gruff despite a tinge of something deeper. "We figured you two were gone for sure."

The wagon master paused, then continued. "Your wife is okay too?"

"She's alive."

Jack understood the emotion simmering beneath the inquiry. It was the moment when you'd lost too much and couldn't bear to lose another person or thing, no matter how small. He explained how they'd found Running Deer and managed to make their way back to the group.

A Journey for Amelia

"I'm glad." The old man's expression grew serious. "But I have to tell you, Jack, we had to leave your wagon behind. The storm shattered it to pieces."

His heart faltered. Sure, he'd kept a few possessions in the wagon, but what he really needed to know was what happened to Bullet.

"What about my horse?"

Barnes looked away, hesitating. "We didn't even notice he went missing at first, but one of the boys saw him bolt during the storm. He's alive, but possibly hurt."

"So, where is he now?" Jack's mind raced. He didn't like how he avoided his question.

"Last we saw, he ran off back that direction," Barnes said, pointing off into the distance.

"What?" Heat crept into his neck and his brows narrowed. "You left him? Didn't even try to look?"

Not that he wished for Bullet to be gone, but leaving an animal to suffer like that made his blood boil. Maybe it wasn't as bad as all that. He'd have to see for himself. No question.

"For all we knew the storm got him, and we had no way to coddle an injured gelding after we lost so many of our own. We had to keep moving," the man replied, a permanent frown etched upon his features. "At least this way there's a chance a native might find him and take him in."

"If wolves don't get to him first," he replied, knowing full well the sting in his words.

Kindness went a long way, and he knew he should've been less hard on Barnes, but all he could see was red. He had to leave. To find Bullet.

"I need to search for him," he said firmly. "I won't leave him behind unless he's too injured then I'll say my goodbyes in person."

Barnes gave him a brief pat on the shoulder. "He could be long gone, but if you go, you shouldn't go alone. Take a few of the boys with you."

Jack considered his words. He needed to find Bullet, but risking his life in the process wouldn't help anything. "You have a deal."

"I'll let my men know. Be careful and give up if you don't find him before nightfall. We'll stay in camp longer to give you one day's time."

With a word of thanks, Jack left and made his way back to inform his wife of the plan. His wife. Strange how she'd been nothing more than a payday for him since the start, yet his knee-jerk reaction was to fill her in on his plans.

When he returned to Amelia, he found the women chatting near the back of Mary's wagon. He pulled her aside, excusing themselves to seek a private word.

The more he tried to explain, the tighter her arms crossed and the deeper her scowl.

"So, you're leaving again?" she asked, her voice cracking.

"I have to find Bullet," he replied, hoping she would understand. "I need you to stay here."

"Why can't I go with you?" Her tone grew more heated. "I'm as capable as any of the men here."

Jack sighed. "It's too dangerous. We just got back."

"I can handle myself," she replied.

"I know you can," Jack said. "But this isn't about that. I would blame myself if something happened to you."

A Journey for Amelia

Her expression softened before she turned away, fists clenched at her sides.

"You're always trying to protect me," she said. "But sometimes I want to be the one to help you instead."

"I know," Jack reached out to graze the sides of her arms. "I appreciate that more than you know. But this time, I have to go alone."

Amelia turned back to him, her eyes unreadable. "Fine. Go then."

His stomach ached knowing he'd hurt her, but he had to find Bullet, no matter what it took. And he wouldn't forgive himself if he put her in harm's way in the process.

"I'll be back," he said, his voice firm. "I promise."

Without another word, he turned and walked away, his heart burdened with the weight of his actions.

eight

AMELIA

The land is just an anchor to the sky. Jack's words still echoed in her head as she lay face up atop compressed prairie grass, her skin tickled by the folded green blades as she spread out to watch the stars chase away the day. Amelia wondered how a place so vast and beautiful could be so undeniably cruel.

All the pain and loss weighed heavily, and it showed. Her words had been harsh earlier, and she knew it, but it hadn't stopped her from losing her temper. It's not as though she would've slowed him down any. They'd return to being strangers by year's end, so he shouldn't care what happened to her. She shouldn't care about him either. And yet…somehow the thought of them going their separate ways caused an ache in her chest.

A Journey for Amelia

When Mary had told her that their wagon had been destroyed, along with all their belongings, her world had crumbled for the second time. Part of her felt grateful that Jack had left to find Bullet because she'd cried more than her fair share of tears that evening. Every earthly possession she'd had was gone. Destroyed. No money, no heirlooms, nothing left of her parents. All she had was the burning desire to make it out West.

"Come eat with us, Amelia," Mary called from the other side of the wagon.

"I'll be right there," she said as she pushed herself up and rose to her feet.

Dusting off her clothes, she straightened the folds of her dress and shuffled around to the campfire. Her friend had been kind to take her in and share food and a place to sleep, offering to allow her and Jack to take shelter in the wagon overnight.

She didn't doubt Mary had a kind heart, but part of her wondered if her new friend craved company after losing her family. An ache gripped Amelia as she recalled the terrible losses. In a way, they were all bound together. If they didn't have each other, they'd have no one.

"Amelia, this is Mr. Davis and his son, Henry."

"Pleasure to make your acquaintance." She greeted the portly man with a thick mustache and knelt to wave at the little boy pretending a tree branch was a sword. Henry giggled and lunged forward to stab her with its pointy end.

Reacting quickly, she wrapped her hand around the bent stick nudged against her bodice and groaned. "You got me. I'm wounded!"

The child squealed, grinning as he released his makeshift weapon to scamper back to his dad, hiding behind him while peeking back at her.

"Thank you for making my boy smile," the man said, his tone solemn but his words cheerful.

Mary brushed by her with a pile of plates, pausing to whisper into her ear. "His wife passed during the storm."

She nodded to Mr. Davis to accept his thanks, but her mood fell, and her brow creased at the thought of Henry losing his mother. Even children weren't immune to the pain of the journey westward. While young ones were typically resilient, only God knew what lasting trauma might wind its way around their hearts.

Everyone took a seat around the campfire as Mary dished up supper and passed the plates around. As soon as the stew from her spoon hit her tongue, she closed her eyes and savored the taste. It'd been far too long since her last hot meal. If Jack were there, he'd be enjoying it too, but it was his loss. Lingering frustration bubbled within her as she finished the food.

After eating, she excused herself, offering to rinse the dishes in the river. She made her way toward the water's edge as fiery hues of the setting sun streaked through the sky, signaling the start of night.

A rustle of tall grass and the murmur of a breeze accompanied her every step. Cool air brushed against her cheeks, and she paused to relish its touch. Finishing her path to the river, she knelt and submerged the plates, the clinking of tin breaking the tranquility of her surroundings.

A Journey for Amelia

The river babbled before her, its current whispering secrets into the fading light. The familiar sound brought a sense of solace, like an old friend offering comfort in troubled times. She scrubbed the dishes, their surface meeting the water, creating delicate ripples that echoed the rhythm of the rushing stream.

As she immersed herself in the peaceful moment, an intrusive sound pulled her from her reverie. Footsteps, heavy and purposeful, approached from behind. Startled, Amelia glanced over her shoulder. It was the man who accused Jack, the same individual who'd kicked over their cooking pot in a rage not long ago. The man's features were etched with hard lines and a scowl sat upon his face as he closed the distance between them along the riverbank.

His gaze pierced her, his eyes cold, as if seeking to test the depths of her loyalty. His voice cut through the air like a sharp blade.

"You might want to watch yourself with that Jack fellow," he warned, his tone rough. "He ain't no good."

Amelia's jaw tightened. The nerve of that man to interrupt her to stir up more trouble. A steadiness settled upon her shoulders, and she straightened her posture.

She stood her ground, replying in a voice as tight as his.

"I appreciate your concern, but I suggest you keep your judgments to yourself." Their eyes locked in a silent battle. "Why should I listen to you about my own husband? I don't even know you."

"Your husband," he said, pausing to kick the ground near his feet. "I find it rather funny how I lived in

Independence for years until I got the notion of moving out West…just to find him on the same route. With a mysterious new wife in tow, no less."

"Clearly you don't know him as well as you let on if you think I'm so mysterious." She pulled the plates from the water and stacked them, purposefully avoiding eye contact with the man.

"Being so fresh and all, I wonder how much he told you 'bout his past," he said.

The sneer on his face disgusted her as she stood to leave, gathering the dishes into her arms. "Don't you have something better to do with your time?" Amelia moved to brush past him, but he grabbed her arm.

"He and his posse raided my farm and ruined my livelihood. Greedy, no-good criminals. The lot of 'em," he snapped, his grip still tight.

Nostrils flared, she yanked her arm from his grasp and continued to walk.

"If you had proof he'd have been behind bars by now, but he's here with me," she said, sharply enunciating, venom running beneath the surface of her words.

"You're smug about it now, but I won't let this go. Wait and see."

"Oh, and whoever you are," she said, glancing back with a sharp stare. "Don't ever touch me again, or you'll regret it."

"Like husband, like wife!" he yelled from behind her as she hurried back to camp.

By the time she got back, she was fuming. She'd have to pray for forgiveness that night as her anger took control of her thoughts, imagining all the ways she'd like to get even with such a disgusting, rude man.

Forcing a smile, she stacked the dishes next to Mary's tent and crawled into the back of her wagon.

"Thank you again for letting us stay with you," she called to her through the thin material barrier.

Mary poked her head out and waved her off to bed. "Get some sleep. I'm happy to have you keep me company."

Crawling beneath the quilt her friend left for her, she used a folded blanket as a pillow and turned on her side to get comfortable. Once her body became still, her mind sped up. Despite her hatred of the man, Jack's enemy at the river worried her. She'd defended her husband, but how well did she truly know him?

She'd considered that a few times during their journey. It was as though Jack was two different people. There was the man she knew during their travels and then there was the man with a mysterious past who attracted trouble at every turn.

The Jack she knew was kind. He protected her, respected her, and joked with her. But the way he'd pulled a gun on that man scared her. Perhaps he did it to send a message…to intimidate. Regardless, the way her stomach did flips when she thought of him made her frown.

With closed eyes, she willed herself to sleep, chasing the thoughts of him from her mind. Despite the distraction, her heart ached. She missed home…if only she still had one. If Ma were alive, she would've made Amelia a hot cup of tea and listened while she spilled all her worries. Somehow, she'd always known what to say.

All Amelia had left was her brother, and if he didn't show up when she arrived in Oregon, she'd have no one. Ever since he'd left them to seek out land, her parents had disowned him. But she knew deep down they hadn't stopped caring for each other. If she could reunite with him, everything would work itself out. It had to.

Staking a claim and tending to it wasn't easy; it was possible something could've befallen him. Without her family, she'd come to rely on Jack…what if he'd been hurt too? He'd still not returned from fetching Bullet and the hour grew late.

Her mind aswirl with fear and uncertainty, she folded a hand against her palpitating heart. She let her tears fall one last time for the day, allowing the emotion to flow out of her like the cleansing stream of a waterfall. She knew deep down she'd been wrong to worry, but it was hard. Oh so hard. To let go and trust the Lord. Her whole life she'd been quick to react and easy to worry, but she preferred to deal with it alone, in the dark of night, away from prying eyes.

She prayed, her lips moving but her voice silent. "Forgive me, God. Please let my heart be at ease."

Before she could continue, a nicker from a horse sounded outside the wagon and heavy footsteps approached. Had the man from earlier returned to threaten her? Or worse? She possessed no weapon, but she did hold the element of surprise. If she lay still until provoked, she could fight fiercely with her fists.

The surface beneath her shook as someone hoisted themselves over the back panel and into the bed of the

A Journey for Amelia

wagon. A scent of sweat and leather filled the air, and she clenched her eyes together. When nothing happened for a good minute, she turned her head and squinted, trying to get a look at who shared the space.

Silver rays of moonlight filtered through the wagon's open circle, casting a halo around the silhouette of a man. He removed his hat and gun belt before stretching his muscles as best he could in the limited space.

It was him. It had to be. Even though she couldn't see his features, she knew. A blush crept over her cheeks as she realized she'd been staring, no longer peeking between her lashes. He turned his head right at that moment and stared into her eyes. She gasped.

nine

JACK

Thank God he'd found Bullet in time. He'd discovered his horse perfectly content, nibbling on the grass as if nothing had happened. The animal could've been attacked by predators or claimed by natives if they'd come across the creature.

Jack ran his hands over Bullet, examining him for injuries. To his relief, there were only a few scrapes on his body and a gash on his leg that wasn't too deep but would keep him from carrying anyone on his back for days. He breathed a sigh of relief and gave the animal's neck an affectionate pat as he thanked him for being brave.

Jack hesitated, thinking about Amelia and how she'd reacted when he'd told her about searching for Bullet. He'd been so sure it wouldn't have bothered her to leave

A Journey for Amelia

her behind, but she'd been visibly shaken. Perhaps she'd just been exhausted after their journey back to the wagon train. Taking a deep breath, he started walking back towards camp with Bullet following behind him as he held the reins loosely by his side.

The other men who had come to help were already far ahead on the trail, but he could still make out their figures in the distance. Jack had taken the time to tend the wound while they started back. Now, he continued his pace, knowing he had to get Bullet home safely but at a speed that didn't hurt his animal companion.

The sun shrank toward the horizon, casting less light across the ever-stretching plains. Rose-colored hues dusted the sky and a gentle breeze flitted through the grass beneath his feet. An uneasiness grew within him, but he had no idea why. Glancing around, he saw nothing unusual, so he continued the path. He shook his head and sighed.

He'd seen it all. Jack had experienced his fair share of hardships, tragedies, and losses. In fact, he'd even been the cause of some. He'd turned into a lonely, broke cowboy hopping from job to job until the latest payday fell into his lap. Back in the day, with his old ways, he wouldn't have cared how he got paid. But things were different now. For some reason, Amelia's sad, searching eyes burned themselves into his mind. The look she gave when he left still did something to his gut.

When they arrived back at the camp, most of the wagon train was already asleep. He could make out a few figures that were still up, tending to their horses and preparing bedding for the night. Jack thanked the men for their help and continued toward the wagon they'd been offered for the night.

Jack hesitated when he saw it, considering what might await him. Amelia had been frustrated when he left, so she might not be too pleased to see him. But exhaustion overwhelmed him. He decided to take the chance and stepped forward tentatively, steeling himself before approaching the wagon's entrance.

He peered inside, finding Amelia asleep beneath a quilt, her body still as she lay on her side. The lack of light prevented him from seeing her face, but he attempted to get ready for bed as quietly as possible. Climbing into the wagon, he turned to remove his belt and hat before bending his back then stretching his arms above his head to either side, pushing the muscles to their limit before turning to find a spot to rest.

He stopped. The moonlight he'd been blocking illuminated Amelia's face, the light catching her eyes as she stared straight at him. She gasped when caught, but he tried to put her at ease.

"Bullet is safe," he whispered.

The limited space in the wagon proved a bit uncomfortable as he lay down next to her, careful to set his body on top of the blanket as she rested below it. With his arms folded beneath his head and his boots freshly kicked to the side, he got as comfortable as he could in tight quarters.

"I worried you wouldn't return." She spoke in such a hushed tone he had to strain to listen.

A Journey for Amelia

"Does that mean you aren't angry anymore?"

Amelia huffed. "Frustrated not angry."

He couldn't see the difference, but he listened patiently.

"I'm glad you're safe," she continued. "I have no idea how or why, but I guess I've come to rely on you out here."

Those words sent tingles through his body, the sentiment piercing his hard exterior like an arrow through his chest. Fast and swift. She faced him now, turning from her other side to peer at him as they spoke.

His heart thudded faster, and he glanced down at her. Her eyes were wide, and her lips were full, and kissing her crossed his mind. But he rejected the idea just as quickly. They weren't married, not even courting…they were nothing more than business partners. He wouldn't dishonor her in that way.

Amelia beamed at him, unaware of the warring thoughts within him. Warmth washed over his weary body, and a tender smile tugged at the corners of his lips. He propped himself up on an elbow. In the dim light, he saw vulnerability in her expression—the trust she'd placed in him amidst the uncertainties of their journey. Strength was on his side as he brushed a strand of hair from her cheek. His fingers grazed her skin and she sighed.

"I reckon I've grown accustomed to you as well," he said as his hand rested gently upon her face. "Now get some sleep."

Turning over, he faced away from her and willed his heart to be still. It wasn't like him. Jack wasn't some lovesick boy; he was a man. A man who had no time for a woman.

Yet at that moment, his rough exterior cracked, revealing a vulnerability of his own that he'd long tried to hide. The weight of his past and future uncertainties faded into the background as his heart yearned for something more than the solitary existence he'd grown accustomed to. He closed his eyes, cherishing the memory of Amelia's touch moments before, and allowed himself to drift into a restless sleep.

Soon morning came, rays of light piercing through the slats of wood and taut canopy. Jack stretched his legs and groaned then rolled over to face the warm body lying next to him. Her eyes remained closed. He'd never seen such a beautiful face, and it took every bit of strength in him not to pull her into his arms. Resting a gentle touch on her shoulder, he cleared his throat.

"Good morning."

Amelia blinked and looked up at him, her brows drawing together as she flinched. Had he startled her? Or maybe she regretted the moment they shared last night. A frown tugged at his features as his body stiffened.

Before he had a chance to ask, she sat up and pushed herself to her feet with a mumbled apology. Smoothing her dress with her palms, she climbed down from the wagon and out of his line of sight.

He should've known he'd scare her away. Nothing good came his way too often, especially to a man with his sort of past. Deep down he knew he should ask her directly, but the gruff part of him ignored the logic. Talking about

A Journey for Amelia

feelings never appealed to him much. If she wanted to ignore him, so be it. It didn't bother him one bit.

His brow pinched, and he huffed as he hoisted his body out of the wagon and strode past Amelia busying herself by the fire. Grabbing his jacket from the front seat of the wagon, he swung it on and patted Bullet's side as he strode out of the camp, refusing to look back.

On his way out, he ran into Mary on her way up from the riverbank. She must've woken early. He tilted his head in greeting. "Mary."

"Jack," she replied as they paused their stride to greet each other. "A lovely morning today, isn't it?"

"Mmm," he mumbled in response as he glanced up into the vast blue expanse above.

"Something on your mind?"

Jack paused before answering. He wasn't sure if he should confide in the woman, but who better to understand a woman's mood than another woman? And Mary seemed to be a good listener.

"It's Amelia," he said, looking down at the ground.

"What about her?" Mary asked, concern etched on her face.

"I...told her some things last night, but this morning she's acting cold toward me," Jack said, his voice uncertain.

Mary patted his shoulder and cleared her throat. "Maybe she needs to process it all. Give her some space and she'll come around."

Jack nodded, but he couldn't shake the heaviness growing in his gut. He'd been so sure that Amelia felt the same way, but maybe he'd misread the signs. Perhaps they'd rushed their feelings due to the dangers they'd experienced. He turned to Mary, grateful for her willingness to advise him even after all she'd been through herself. "Thanks," he said, a small weight lifted off his back. "I'll do that."

The earthy scent of campfires mingled with the crisp air as morning turned toward noon, and he ventured closer to the outskirts of the camp in his walk, his mind immersed in a whirlwind of thoughts. He sought solace in solitude, yearning to unwind from the earlier web of emotion.

Passing by the wagon master's tent, a cacophony of voices reached his ears, their raised tones drifting through the fabric walls. The heavy mood gnawed at him, drawing him closer to the source of the commotion. He paused, frowning, his hand lingering on the edge of the tent's flap. The heated exchange of words piqued his interest to a point impossible to ignore.

With a deep exhale, he pushed the heavy fabric aside, the slight resistance of the material offering a brief time to turn back but he pushed forward. Shadows danced along the fabric walls, cast by the dim light of a flickering lantern. The figures within the tent engaged in a passionate exchange.

Voices clashing, a timber of anger tinged the air, intermingled with a damp scent that hung heavy in the confined space. Jack scanned the room, taking in the faces distorted by desperation. His gaze settled on the wagon master, his weathered features etched with deep lines.

The leader of their journey wiped the sweat from his reddened cheeks as he argued with a tall,

A Journey for Amelia

broad-shouldered man next to him. Jack recognized him as one of the guides they'd hired before departing.

"What's going on here?" Jack demanded, stepping inside.

The guide turned to him, his eyes flashing. "We need to cross that river, and we need to do it now. We can't wait any longer."

Jack shook his head. "It's too dangerous. The river's deep and fast-moving."

"We've got no choice," the guide insisted. "Our supplies won't last. We need to cross no later than tomorrow if we wish to resupply at the nearest fort."

Jack sighed and rubbed his hands over his face, the weight of the situation pressing down on him. They couldn't lead these people to their deaths, but if they didn't try, a slower death awaited them by starvation.

"We're going to lose some people," Jack said.

"We've lost so many already. You've got some nerve, entering my tent uninvited," Mr. Barnes replied in a harsh tone.

"I know you don't trust me, but I've seen these plains more than anyone with all the cattle I've escorted over the years." Jack stared straight ahead. "If anyone can help these people cross, it's me."

"And me," the guide stated, stepping up shoulder to shoulder beside Jack.

The wagon master threw up his hands and sighed.

"Alright, you win," he grumbled. "Not as though we have many options. Go tell the other men to prepare while I work out a plan."

Willow Callaway

As he left the tent and meandered back toward camp, his mind churned, echoing the turmoil of the river they were set to cross. The river—a treacherous obstacle that could claim lives without mercy. Jack had witnessed its power before and seen the lives it had swallowed whole. It was an unforgiving force, judging anyone who dared to defy its depths.

He made a few stops to help families prepare their wagons, ropes, and supplies for the journey across the water. Insisting each person recite the steps to secure their bodies and possessions during the crossing kept him busy, but soon he let his footsteps lead him back over a familiar path. The others could take over for now.

Memories flooded his mind, the haunting images of rushing currents and desperate struggles. He could almost hear roaring water still echoing in his ears, a reminder of the fate that lay ahead.

Jack trudged through the camp and approached Amelia as she sat by the fire, her head bowed. He hesitated, but he knew he had to try to make things right before the crossing. As he drew closer, he noticed the way her shoulders trembled, as if holding back tears.

"Amelia," he said, "I'm sorry about last night. I didn't mean to scare you."

She looked up at him, her eyes red-rimmed and puffy.

"I know," she whispered. "I'm scared. About the river. The rest of the journey. You and me. Just…everything."

She knew. He silently cursed the fact that word had spread before he could tell her himself, but he should've

A Journey for Amelia

expected it after his slow walk back to the wagon. Jack knelt beside her, taking her hand in his.

"I understand," he said, trying to keep his own voice steady. "But we'll get through this. Together."

"Like the storm." Amelia said, her eyes fixed on his. Something passed between them in that moment, a sense of understanding that went beyond words. Unfortunately, it was short-lived as her anxiety weighed down around them.

"How do you know for sure?" She glanced past his shoulder, toward the direction of the river.

"Nothing in this life is certain, Amelia, except for God and this wild land. We live, we love, we die."

"If you're trying to make me feel better, it isn't working," she said.

"The realities of life aren't made for comfort. But what I can promise you is that I won't leave your side."

The moment the words left his lips, his heart clenched. On the surface, it meant he'd help her cross the river, but without realizing when it changed, somehow his words ran deeper. He yearned to be by her side as long as he could. To protect her beyond the job and after reaching their destination.

He pushed the thought aside, closing his eyes to exhale. "What's for dinner?"

"You think I cooked at a time like this? You've lost your marbles," she said, taking the opportunity to run with the topic change as she sniffled and wiped her stray tears. "Jack."

"You know I'm no good at cooking if that's what you're asking," he said with a grin.

"It's not that," she replied, a wrinkle of concern lacing her brow again as she stood.

He swallowed and steeled himself. Was she still angry with him?

"I— " her question cut short as a scream echoed through the camp.

ten

AMELIA

The loud screeching sound pierced the air, and Amelia pressed a hand to her chest as her words stumbled.

"Wait here," Jack commanded before rushing off toward the commotion.

Of course, he would tell her not to follow. Now she was the one who wanted to scream but forced herself to hold it in. Every time they bonded, something would happen, or a nagging doubt would arise.

There was no way she'd wait. She trailed behind him, unable to keep up with his longer strides. Deciding against asking him to slow down, she traveled at her own pace through the wagon train, keeping an eye on his form in the distance.

Her mind drifted to the night before when they'd shared a moment. She could still feel the warmth of his frame next to hers as they'd lain in a wagon beneath the stars. Caught up in the moment, Amelia had nearly succumbed to her desire to give her heart away, but the next morning reality came crashing down. Despite her intuition, she knew Jack could be dangerous. She'd needed to push him away, to protect herself.

An eerie quiet settled over the camp as she walked between wagons, a stark contrast to the usual lively atmosphere. The chatter of tired travelers exchanging stories and laughter was gone, replaced by the heavy silence that covered the area like a shroud. Families clung to one another in a tight embrace, the wind whipping their hair and clothes. Tears cascaded down some of their cheeks, while others donned expressions void of emotion, their vision fixed on a distant horizon.

The air hung heavy with a bittersweet aroma, a poignant blend of wood and the remnants of freshly cooked supper. The fading embers of the campfires released a wispy trail of fragrant smoke that drifted lazily through the air, weaving its way into the depths of her nostrils. The scent carried memories now tinged with melancholy. It clung to her senses, a reminder of the unity that had once bound them when they began their journey, now overshadowed by loss both in the past and future.

A second scream turned into a mournful wail, traveling over the wagon tops to reach her ears. Hurrying her pace, she caught up to Jack who stood before a tight circle of people a few feet out from one of the wagons.

A Journey for Amelia

"He took my baby boy. He's gone!" A woman yelled, her words mangled by sobs as she begged and pleaded. She'd fallen to her knees, grasping at the legs of anyone who listened.

Amelia's heart plummeted as the woman's grief consumed her. She knew all too well how it felt to lose a loved one. The pain never truly faded, but it became bearable with time. Her chest tightened as she made her way to the woman, kneeling beside her and placing a hand on her shaking back.

"Tell us who took your child," she murmured, wrapping her arm further around the woman in a comforting embrace.

She continued to sob, her body wracked with grief. Amelia looked over to Jack, searching for any sign of what they should do. Jack's jaw was set as he scanned the area.

"My husband took him. We fought, and he left with our son," she replied, tears streaming down her face.

Her heart ached for the woman. She knew how things could escalate between lovers on the trail. The constant danger, the lack of resources, and the uncertainty could drive even the most loving of couples to their breaking point.

"He may return. Perhaps he needed to clear his head," Amelia said but struggled to believe her own words. It didn't look good.

"We fought about the river crossing," the woman said between sniffles. "I wanted to cross, but he insisted it'd be safer to turn around and go home."

There was no way he'd make it back, but Amelia knew better than to bring it up right then. She imagined how hopeless the woman must've felt to see her family disappear without her.

Some of the men gathered around promised her they'd look for her missing loved ones. A dark look in Jack's eyes told her it likely wouldn't end well, but the assurance from the others calmed the woman's hysterics.

"It's going to be okay," she consoled her. "Can you tell us which way he went?"

The grieving mother pointed behind her with a shaky hand.

Amelia and Jack helped the woman to her feet, offering their support as they guided her to a nearby empty spot. Together, they worked to set up a temporary tent for her, using spare blankets and ropes from the wagons. Amelia's hands moved with practiced ease, tying knots, and securing the fabric to create a small shelter. She'd always been handy growing up thanks to Pa's guidance.

As they worked, their voices whispered words of reassurance, promising the woman that they'd do everything in their power to help her find her son and restore her family.

Once the tent was erected, the woman stepped inside, her sobs turned to whimpers. Amelia patted her shoulder, offering what little comfort she could amidst the turmoil.

"Don't give up hope," Amelia said, her voice soft but firm. "We'll do our best."

The woman blinked, her tear-streaked face tinged pink from her sobs. Amelia exchanged a glance with Jack, a silent understanding passing between them.

A Journey for Amelia

As they left the woman's temporary shelter, Amelia's energy drained from her body. A temporary high from caring for the woman disappeared after her emotions settled. The tense atmosphere in the camp intensified, mirroring the heaviness in her heart. The upcoming river crossing loomed large in her mind, a treacherous obstacle that threatened to wash away their hopes and dreams. Morale was low around camp with a lot of dangers come morning, yet somehow, they had to gather enough manpower and heart to start a search party.

Thoughts of the strong river currents haunted her as she and Jack made their way back to their wagon. Their footsteps echoed hollowly in the silence. The weight of their earlier dispute still lingered, and a subtle tension hung in the air between them. An increasing darkness with only a pale moon to light their path seemed to amplify the unease, casting a dim glow over the dirt as they walked.

Amelia climbed into the wagon, settling onto the makeshift bed they'd prepared. Jack didn't follow but instead leaned against the wood panels. She sensed his turmoil, just as her own worries consumed her.

"Get some sleep. I'll be back by morning," Jack said.

She sighed. "I hope you find them."

"Several men are already trying to track him. I needed to walk you back first but will catch up to the group."

Amelia wanted to argue, but she stopped herself. She realized she was glad he escorted her back. Despite hating to admit it, she was afraid.

"Take these," she said, grabbing a few of the biscuits left from breakfast, which had been wrapped in a handkerchief and set aside. "You haven't eaten all day."

The flickering lantern cast a dim glow within the wagon, its warming light painting the wooden walls pale gold. He reached out to take the offering and thanked her.

"Be safe." She bid him farewell and lay down.

Amelia rested as his footsteps faded, but sleep evaded her. The image of the distraught woman's face, filled with desperation and longing, haunted her thoughts. She wondered if they could fulfill their promise to help her and if they could navigate the treacherous river to emerge unscathed on the other side.

As the night wore on, sleep claimed Amelia, but her dreams were restless, filled with swirling currents and dark waters. She tossed and turned, her mind repeating the events of the day and the uncertainty of what lay ahead.

The distant sound of the flowing river seemed to echo in her ears, a siren call luring her down the bank and into the cold, black water. Her legs moved unbidden, taking her deeper and deeper until the water reached her chin, snaking over her lips, down her throat, and into her lungs. She coughed and gasped for air. As her world turned black, her eyes snapped open.

Beads of sweat lined her forehead, and her chest heaved as she sat up. Another nightmare. A sigh of relief escaped as a gentle touch grazed her arm.

"Amelia?" Jack peered at her in the dim light of the wagon, his brow folded and mouth downturned.

A Journey for Amelia

"You're back."

"You were breathing erratically in your sleep; you had me worried."

"I'm glad it was just a dream," she said but in the back of her mind, she worried about bad omens. Pushing it down she reminded herself to trust in God. "Did you find that woman's family?"

Jack paused as if considering her quick change of subject before answering. "We did, but…her husband refused to return."

"So, you came back empty-handed?" she asked, turning to him.

"No, we were able to get her son," he said, leaning back and propping an arm between his head and the worn boards.

"He was willing to let him go?"

"We didn't give him much choice, facing down the barrels of our guns." He glanced at her then averted his eyes.

"Why not force him back then?" Amelia swallowed as she stared, waiting for a reply.

"More trouble than it's worth to force a grown man. The boy wasn't given a choice in the matter when his dad took him. Kept crying for his mother when we found the lad." He shrugged.

"So sad seeing families torn apart. Some lost to sickness, others to discord. Will it ever end?" The question was rhetorical, but her heart ached all the same and longed for an answer.

Silence stretched between them as Jack got ready and lay down. In some ways, she appreciated that he didn't lie to her. They both knew the situation was dire. Some wouldn't make it across tomorrow. Every day their numbers dwindled. Amelia longed for the time before her parents passed. Before her brother left. Back on the farm with the wind blowing through her hair as she ran down to the creek to collect mushrooms. The simple, unspoiled joys of youth.

With the lingering memories of her childhood, sleep claimed her once more. She welcomed a good rest since the journey had plagued her with nightmares, and the next morning wouldn't bring much relief as they faced raging waters and a fate she dared not dwell upon.

eleven

AMELIA

The morning sun rose, its rays peeking into the wagon to illuminate the space with a steady warmth. Amelia shifted and rubbed her eyes before sitting up to face the world. To face the river. She sighed then folded the blanket and stacked it with the rest of their things.

Jack was already up, busying himself with preparations for the river crossing. His strong hands worked deftly, coiling rope, and preparing Bullet for the journey. He moved about the campsite, double-checking the supplies they'd need. The rhythm of his movements calmed her nerves, making her feel safe and secure. She knew he had her back, no matter what. The uncertainty of their future made her heart hurt, but she pushed it aside. This wasn't the time to be thinking about such things. They had to make it across the river first.

As she stood up to stretch her legs, Jack turned towards her, and their eyes met. She could sense his gaze on her, warm and inviting. She knew he wanted to say something, but instead, he smiled at her.

The way he looked at her melted her cold exterior. It may not have been the time to confess, but she wondered…what if they never got a second chance.

Amelia took a deep breath, gathering courage to speak the truth. "Jack, I know we've been through a lot together on this trail," she said, her voice hesitant. "And I know I've been holding back, but I need to tell you something."

A flicker of concern crossed his face. "What is it, Amelia? Is everything okay?"

Amelia took another deep breath, gathering her thoughts. "I know it might sound crazy, but I care about you. I keep wanting to give in to whatever this is," she said, motioning between them. "But I don't know you. Not truly. You're a walking mystery. I can trust you with my life but not my heart. Not yet."

Jack's expression softened, and he stepped closer to her. "Amelia, I…"

Before he could finish, the wagon master cleared his throat from behind them. Amelia blushed and turned away, embarrassed after pouring out her feelings.

Mr. Barnes stood there with his arms crossed, a stern expression on his weathered face. "I hate to interrupt your little chat, but we need to get moving," he said gruffly, his

A Journey for Amelia

eyes darting back and forth between the two of them. "The river waits for no one."

Jack nodded and turned back to her, his hand reaching out to touch her arm. "We'll talk about this later, okay?" he said, sliding his grip down to her hand and squeezing gently. "Right now, we have to focus on getting across that river."

Amelia agreed, heat still tinging her cheeks. She didn't know what to think about his response. Was he trying to deflect the situation, or did he really mean they would talk later? She pushed the thought aside and focused on the task at hand.

Together, they finished packing up the meager belongings donated to them since the storm and joined the rest of the wagon train headed down to the water. As they approached the riverbank, she trembled. She'd never seen a river that wide before. The sound of the rushing water was overwhelming, and she feared whether they'd make it across.

They joined a line of wagons, all waiting to cross. The water rushed by, cold and unforgiving, and a sense of dread flowed through Amelia. The strong current and deep waters could easily sweep away a wagon and its occupants. This was it. This was the moment they'd all been preparing for.

Mr. Barnes barked orders. "If you haven't already, unload everything but the essentials," he yelled. "We can't risk taking too much weight across the river."

People groaned and grumbled as they began to unload excess items. Some were angry, having already been forced to leave many of their possessions behind. But Amelia knew it was necessary. They had to do their part.

As they helped Mary unload a few more items from the back of her wagon, a hand grazed Amelia's shoulder where it stopped to rest. She turned to see Jack with a familiar, determined look on his face.

"We'll make it across," he said, his voice gentle. "I promise."

Amelia took comfort in his words. She knew that Jack would do everything in his power to make that happen. He walked over to Bullet, patting the horse's neck and whispering something in his ear. She knew that Bullet was more than a means of transportation to Jack. He was a trusted companion.

Once they were finished, they joined the line of people waiting to cross the river. Tension lingered in the air as they stood, waiting for their turn. The cool water rushed by, sending shivers down her spine. Waiting and watching each wagon enter the river, she held her breath every time someone went a little too deep. She reminded herself to stay calm, exhaling a deep breath and praying. Jack took Bullet across on his first trip then traveled back and forth to help many people cross.

She heard someone shout, and she turned her head to see a wagon, pulled by oxen, being swept downstream. The other travelers wailed and splashed, struggling through the water with no time to mourn as the river stopped for no man. They had to move faster. They had to get across.

A Journey for Amelia

Jack had already returned to help the stranded travelers. He was a blur of motion, jumping from one wagon to another, trying to save anyone he could from the river's clutches.

When he made it back to their side of the river, he handed them the end of a rope that stretched across to the opposite bank. "Go ahead. Mind your step, and don't you dare let go. I'll be right behind you."

Amelia clung to the rope, her knuckles turning white. Tears streaked down her face and Mary's whole body shook. The image of the overturned wagon burned into her mind, and she could still hear the screams echoing in her head. The water rushed around her ankles as she stepped forward, sending chills down her spine. She looked back at Jack, who was leading Mary's wagon through the water.

Amelia gripped the rope tighter as the water soaked through her clothes. The wagons swayed in the strong current as the oxen struggled to maintain their footing. Amelia held on tight, praying that they wouldn't be swept away.

She glanced back to see Jack's muscles tense as he steered the wagon through the rushing water. His face held a hard expression of focus, and Amelia wished she was there by his side.

They made it halfway across when disaster struck. The wagon hit a large rock, causing it to tilt precariously.

Amelia's body froze as the wagon swayed and almost tipped. She could hear Mary's screams as she clutched onto her tightly. Jack climbed down from the front of the wagon, his face contorted, and his body strained as he pulled hard to steady it.

"Jack, what do we do?" Amelia shouted, her voice barely audible over the roar of the water.

"Keep going!" Jack yelled back. "I've got this."

That stubborn, ridiculous man. There was no way Amelia would let him struggle against the wagon alone in dangerous waters. Jack tried to step over the rope tied between the wagon and the other side, but his foot caught sending him sprawling face-first into the water. Fear like no other tore through her and she jumped into action.

"Mary, follow the rope. I'm going back for him!" She yelled to her friend, pointing to the opposite shore as she turned to go. A freezing, clammy hand clamped onto her forearm.

"Don't leave me, Amelia," she wailed, tears turning into sobs as she begged her to stay. "I'm afraid."

"I have to go," she insisted, pulling her arm from her friend's grip to press forward toward the wagon. With every step, she fought against the current. The roar of the water grew louder in her ears as she traversed the uneven riverbed as water splashed into her eyes and up her nose. Where was he? Please, God, don't let him still be under.

"Amelia!"

Mary's pleas sounded more like muffled whispers as she inched closer to the wagon. Suddenly they stopped. Had she reached the riverbank? She glanced behind but her friend was nowhere to be seen. She must've been among the crowd on the other side, huddled together beneath blankets.

A Journey for Amelia

Despite the passing thought, she hadn't slowed her pace, pushing as hard as possible through the raging currents pulling at her body. Amelia was a fighter. She'd always been a fighter. As a child she'd run wild all day, climbing trees, swimming in the creek, and horseback riding until sundown. One river wouldn't stop her, especially when Jack needed her most.

Upon reaching where he'd fallen into the water, Amelia dove into the river, keeping one hand gripped to the rope. Scouring the depths with her free hand, she explored until her fingers bumped into his hard frame. Her pulse raced as she felt around to see if she could help…to see if he was still alive. She plunged herself under the water.

Without being upright, the heavy current made it impossible for him to right himself. The pressure of the water beat down over him as his hands flew around his leg in hurried motions. The rope had tangled tight around his ankle like a noose at the gallows. She settled her palms over his hands to calm him then pushed his frenzied actions aside so she could take over.

Determined as ever, she worked fervently to unknot the rope and set him free, letting her nimble fingers and senses guide her movements. She looped the rope down over his foot and pushed his leg free with her hand. Grabbing his body, she hugged him tight around the waist and pushed upward with all her might, sending them bursting through the surface, gasping for air.

Amelia sighed in relief when the sound of Jack coughing up water reached her ears. She patted him on the back and pressed the loose rope into his hands. They clung to each other for balance and took a moment to steady themselves.

"I thought I'd lost you!" she shouted, tears lining her eyes as the river splashed around their waists.

The two of them made the rest of the way across the river with the wagon. Once everything had been dragged onto dry land, she collapsed onto the grass, hugging her knees to her chest as every ounce of energy drained from her body, equalizing after the rush of adrenaline.

Jack approached her with an extra blanket and dropped it over her shoulders. Sitting down in front of her, he touched her arm, and she looked up to meet his eyes.

"I have something to tell you," he said with a slight frown.

"I'm just glad you're okay. When I saw you'd lost your balance I froze. I-" She spoke in a jumble.

"Amelia, please." Jack placed both hands on her shoulders, squeezing softly.

"I know you're usually the one who saves me, but this time I was able to help."

"It's Mary," he said firmly.

"What do you mean?" There was something about the look on his face she didn't like. Swallowing hard, she blinked a few times to recenter her thoughts, but he kept speaking.

"She…didn't make it."

"What? No!" Amelia shouted. "She was right beside me. She made it to shore."

"Did you see that?"

A Journey for Amelia

"No, I mean...I assumed. She's got to be here. We need to look again." Her head bobbed back and forth as she scanned the crowd.

"They saw her lose her footing while you were on your way to help me."

"It's my fault. It's all my fault." Amelia hugged her knees and swayed as her nausea rose. He was wrong. He had to be.

"You didn't know...you had no way of knowing," he repeated. "The river is relentless, and you can't hear a thing over its roar."

"She begged me not to go," she said, her voice cracking.

"You had to make a difficult choice."

"I should've been able to save you both."

"Forgive yourself. Don't allow guilt to darken your heart." He cupped her face in his hands, allowing his thumbs to wipe away her tears.

Life on the road had finally gotten to her. All the loss, the pain, the exhaustion. She let go and allowed her pain to settle without reprieve. More tears flowed, streaking down her crimson-tinged face in rivulets to settle in the crook of her neck as she sniffled. Heat rose beneath her skin and her body felt clammy to the touch. Her chest heaved with every sob, rising and falling in quick succession.

Jack released her face and drew her into his arms to hold her tight. The top of her head was tucked beneath his chin as he ran his hand across her back in a soothing circular motion. Something about his frame wrapped around hers made her feel safe. She could almost forget the nightmare of the day, if only briefly.

Time passed slowly and the world seemed to blur. The last thing Amelia remembered was those strong familiar arms lifting her from the ground and carrying her out of the crowd and toward the wagon. As her head fell back, too tired to hold it steady any longer, her sight locked on the raging river behind them. The gnashing, angry jaws of water continued to flow without remorse for the lives it'd taken. It was cruel. The wilderness was cruel. And with that thought, everything faded to black as exhaustion overtook her frail body.

twelve

JACK

Days turned to weeks, and weeks to months, as they journeyed on the arduous trail. Amelia's grief remained a heavy burden, casting a shadow over her spirit. With each passing day, Jack observed her growing weaker, her laughter fading, and her once vibrant eyes losing their spark. It was as if a part of her had drowned along with Mary in the river that fateful day.

One morning, as the sun rose high overhead, Jack found Amelia sitting alone by the campfire, staring into the dwindling flames with a distant look on her face. His brows pushed low, he approached with a gentle gait.

"Amelia," he said, settling down beside her. "You should eat something."

She merely nodded, her gaze remaining fixed on the dancing embers. Grief had taken its toll, leaving her unresponsive.

"You can't go on like this," he urged, his voice strained. "You need to forgive yourself."

His words elicited a faint flicker in her spirit, but she remained silent. Jack sighed, trying to find the right words to reach her wounded heart.

"You see," he began, searching for a way to make her understand, "We all carry burdens from our past. In fact, I used to blame myself for what happened to my sister."

Amelia turned toward him, an eyebrow raised. Despite her grief, she seemed drawn into his words. Perhaps he could break through the walls she'd built around herself with a little more effort.

"I was barely grown then," Jack continued, his voice softening with the memory. "My sister married a marshal, and at first, we all believed he was a good man. But as time went on, he showed his true colors. He was abusive, and I blamed myself for not seeing the signs…for not protecting her. For not saving her life."

Amelia's brow furrowed as she listened to Jack's painful confession. He wondered if she sensed the weight of guilt on his shoulders, much like the burden she carried.

"But you were still young," she said.

Jack's eyes reflected the scars of the past. "I know that now. But for the longest time, I couldn't forgive myself. It ate away at me, just as your grief does the same."

For a moment, silence hung between them, heavy with unspoken emotions.

A Journey for Amelia

"You can't change what happened," Jack said. "But you can choose how you carry it. You don't have to bear this burden alone."

Her tears welled up, breaking through the walls she'd erected. She turned to Jack, emotions running high.

"By God's grace, we survived, Amelia. Now we must honor that second chance the Lord gave us. Honor those we've lost by living our lives to the fullest. Mary would want you to keep going."

"Thank you," she whispered, her voice trembling. "I don't know how to let go."

"You don't have to do it all at once," Jack reassured her, placing a comforting hand on her shoulder. "Take it one step at a time."

He patted her on the arm. The discomfort in his stomach remained even though Amelia didn't pry for more answers. Even bringing up his sister soured his gut. It felt like forever ago and yesterday all at the same time.

With tensed muscles, Jack stood up and dusted off his trousers. He couldn't linger on the past, not when they had so far to go. The journey ahead would be long and treacherous, and they couldn't afford to fall behind. He turned to Amelia, offering her a small smile.

"Come on now," he said, extending his hand to her. "Let's pack up and hit the trail."

Amelia accepted his hand as he helped her to her feet. They set to work, readying the wagon for another day. As they loaded the wagon and prepared to travel, Amelia turned to Jack with a curious look.

"May I ask you something?" she inquired tentatively.

"Of course."

"What happened after your sister died? I mean, you said you blamed yourself for not protecting her, but what happened after that?"

Jack's features hardened, and his eyes grew distant. "Those were dark years," he said, his voice low. "When the law failed me, I abandoned the law in return."

"Did...you hurt people?" she asked in a hushed tone.

He recoiled as if she'd slapped him. "Is that what you think of me?"

"No! I—" she said, stumbling over her words.

"I've stolen, I've been on the run, but I've never hurt a soul. Even when I wanted to."

He'd been plenty tempted to harm the man who took his sister from him, but he'd refrained. Barely. Yet causing havoc up and down the marshal's territory with a band of outlaws had given him a small sense of twisted justice. The problem was that once the rage subsided it wasn't so easy to get out of the bandit life. He'd made amends with the Lord, but his old crew didn't take kindly to his leaving. Every day he expected them to show up. He knew them well enough to know how deeply they held a grudge.

As they settled into their day of travels, the wagon rolled farther into the wilderness and a sense of unease settled over Jack. Amelia hadn't said a word after his explanation, but he didn't have it in him to push the topic, welcoming a comfortable silence.

Glancing beyond the wagons, he scanned the horizon for anything unusual. Rehashing his old life brought his

A Journey for Amelia

paranoia rushing back. But his fears were unlikely to be true. He'd taken Amelia's deal for a reason, so they couldn't be following him still. Impossible. He scanned the horizon again and he frowned.

There, in the distance, a thick plume of smoke rose into the sky. Jack's heart quickened in his chest. A fire could mean anything on the plains, but he couldn't shake the feeling that it was a bad sign.

He glanced over at Amelia, but she seemed lost in thought, her eyes distant and unfocused. He didn't want to worry her, so he kept the concerns to himself and focused on the task at hand.

As the sun began to dip below the horizon, the wagon train made camp for the night. Amelia set to work preparing their meager meal while Jack readied their fire.

The evening grew late, and they sat down for their meal, the other members of the group chatting and laughing, their voices carrying on the breeze. But Jack couldn't relax.

After supper, he busied himself around camp while Amelia turned in early for the night. Stoking the fire and adding enough wood to keep it burning, he stood up and stretched his muscles, his bones cracking as he leaned backward. It relaxed his aching joints, and he exhaled only to stop breathing the moment cold steel dug into his spine.

"Shout a single word and you're a dead man."

"Not again," he hissed as he glanced behind, recognizing the man who'd been a thorn in his side the whole trip. Old Joe McCallan.

The assailant, clearly drunk, swayed unsteadily on his feet. "I told you I'd make you pay," he slurred, waving his gun around before poking it back into Jack's flesh.

His hand searched for his own gun, but his heart sank with the realization that he'd left it in the wagon. He was defenseless against Joe's drunken rage.

"What do you want?" Jack asked, trying to keep his voice calm and steady.

"I want you gone," Joe spat, his breath reeking of whiskey. "I want you out of this camp now and out of my sight."

"I can't," he replied as he turned around to face the man. "I have people relying on me to guide them through this journey. We can't pack up and leave."

"Then I guess you'll have to die," he sneered, raising the gun, and pressing it into Jack's temple.

"It doesn't have to be like this. We can talk about it like men," he said, trying to reason with him.

"Talk? You think I want to talk to you?" Joe asked. "You took everything from me."

"We barely took anything that day."

"Is that what your friends told you?" he scoffed. "They took it all. Every last bit."

The corners of Jack's mouth turned down as he mulled over his words.

"Your wife will find your lifeless body, never getting to say goodbye." Spit flew from his mouth as he snarled.

He cocked the gun and perspiration lined Jack's spine. A flash of movement caught his eye to the left as a mess of fabric and hair rushed forward. A cracking sound echoed as Amelia slammed a small rock against the back of Joe's head, causing him to stumble and the gun to slip from his hands.

Grateful for her intervention, Jack wasted no time diving for the weapon. Grabbing its hilt, he pulled it up from the ground and gripped it then aimed at his assailant. The stubby man with the ragged beard and wild eyes gripped his head where he'd been hit, groaning.

"Pack your wagon and be gone by morning." With the direction of the gun now reversed, Jack spoke slowly but sharply. "If I see your face again, I promise you'll regret it."

Disoriented and defeated, the man scurried off like a frightened rat, tripping over his own feet in his haste to get away.

Jack watched him go, lowered the gun, and then turned to Amelia. A sense of calm flooded his body. The petite woman before him had come to his aid, but a heaviness still hung in the air between them.

Though pale and trembling, she stood tall. He could tell it'd all been too much for her, but she was too proud to break. Her eyes were dry despite her usual propensity for tears and her hands were balled into two tight fists.

He couldn't help but worry. Somehow through all their highs and lows, he still cared. And he hated himself for it. She seemed to want nothing to do with him. Amelia had been withdrawn for months.

"Are you okay?" he asked, approaching her slowly so as not to startle her.

"I-I think so," she said, blinking a few times before looking up. "What'll you do to him if he doesn't leave?"

He stood still, considering her question. "Well, what he thinks I'll do to him is far more important than what I'd actually do."

Amelia still looked shaken. "I don't know how much more of this I can take," she whispered, her voice blending with the sounds of nightfall on the plains.

"What do you mean?" he asked.

"I mean all of this," she gestured around them. "The danger, the uncertainty. I thought I was ready, but I'm starting to wonder."

Jack studied her, his heart aching at the sight of her trembling form. He wanted to reach out to her, to hold her and tell her that everything would be alright, but he knew he shouldn't. There'd been too many secrets and too many hardships to repair.

Instead, he spoke carefully, "Everyone gets scared sometimes. We've come this far, it's too late to turn back now."

Amelia nodded, her vision downcast. "I know, but it's…all too much." She took a deep breath and looked up at him, her gaze searching. "Do you ever regret coming on this journey, Jack?"

He paused, considering his answer. "No, I don't regret it. It's been hard, harder than I ever could've imagined, but…" He trailed off, searching for the right words. "It's worth it, Amelia. It's worth it for the chance to start a new life."

She looked at him for a long moment. "I hope you're right," she said. "I want to believe that it'll all be worth it in the end."

"It will be," he said firmly, reaching out to touch her arm. "I promise."

They stood in silence, his heart beating strong against his ribs. Then Amelia pulled away, her face tired and expression unreadable.

"What is it?" he asked, studying her every move.

"I'm going to get some sleep."

She climbed into the wagon and readied herself to turn in for the night. He exhaled and set about tidying the camp as thoughts flooded his mind.

Over the past couple of months, he'd tried to move on from Amelia. Every time he came close to success, she'd light up the night with her laugh, patch another hole in his pants while humming the most beautiful tune, or smash a man's head with a rock. Despite her pain, she never ceased to shine.

If he hadn't known for sure Amelia was a God-fearing woman, he'd have been positive the devil had bewitched him. The corners of his lips inclined as a breeze flitted through his short, tangled hair.

After a while he joined her in the wagon, settling next to her with his ears alert and his eyes glued to the exit. Tuning out the cicadas' symphony, he listened intently for any disturbances. If Joe returned, he'd be ready.

thirteen

AMELIA

Amelia lay beneath the blanket, her eyelids heavy but her mind still wide awake. The last few months had been a blur, her emotions reaching lows she hadn't felt since her parents passed. Every time she dared to hope, everything was stripped away from her.

Jack had been the one to pull her from the darkness once again. She'd allowed herself to become a victim of loss, and some days she longed to quit and return home. But they'd traveled too far to turn back. Part of healing was accepting those losses and pushing forward.

Heavy breathing drew her focus to her husband, fast asleep beside her. He'd stayed awake for a long while, staring out the back of the wagon, but eventually, his exhaustion won the battle between wakefulness and sleep. His

A Journey for Amelia

face looked relaxed without a stern expression or the fine lines of worry that often crossed his forehead.

Her hand almost reached out to ghost along his cheek, but she stopped herself. Amelia understood he probably found her closed off and reclusive since Mary's passing. Honestly, it wasn't that she hated him, it was that she hated herself for wanting him.

Pulling the quilt further up beneath her chin, she sighed. Jack had always been there for her through every difficulty they'd faced on the trail. Yet she couldn't shake the thought of him using violence. Would he have hurt that nasty man, Joe?

Deep down she knew the real issue. Fear. She was afraid to let someone in and lose them. Loss after loss had left her afraid to love. Afraid to lose anyone else.

There was time. She reminded herself she didn't have to decide today. Allowing her eyes to flutter closed, she welcomed sleep, and a pleasant memory of her family surrounded her, pulling her deeper into slumber.

Suddenly she jolted awake. How long had she been out? The sky outside shone bright with stars, but wailing screams and gunshots filled the air. Men shouted from beyond the wagon, and the spot next to her now lay empty.

Where had Jack gone? Why hadn't he woken her? Amelia's mind spun as she gathered a gun from the wagon and hopped out, trying to recall Jack's lessons on shooting. A woman collided with her as she reached the ground, nearly sending her sprawling. Before she could speak, the lady continued running past her, into the wilderness.

Another gunshot. Then another.

A native attack? No, it didn't sound like it. She readied the rifle and pushed into the center of the circled wagons. Another runner headed straight for her, but this time she was prepared. Grabbing the young man by his wrist, she begged him for answers.

"What happened?"

"Outlaws!"

An instant wave of cold washed over her. "Where?"

"Outside the circle," he said, pointing behind him. "The men went out to fight."

Lord help them. She released the boy's hand and frowned as he made his escape. Most of the people in the wagon train were emigrants or farmers, not fighters. She'd helped Pa a time or two against trespassers, but it'd never come to shots fired. At least a few of the wagon master's men and Jack seemed capable. Jack. Her heart constricted, imagining him in a shoot-out.

That fool would put himself at risk. He hadn't even woken her or said goodbye. Moving to the edge of the circle, she hopped over the wagon chain and ignored the protests of those holed up in the last line of defense along the perimeter.

Chaos enveloped her as she stepped further outside the safety of their wagons. Shouting drowned out the sounds of the night as gunshots continued to echo. The stench of gunpowder filled her nostrils and wild grass whipped against her shins.

A Journey for Amelia

"Jack!" she shouted over the noise, searching for any sign of him amidst the standoff.

"Behind you!" He yelled from beyond a rock a few feet away.

Amelia spun around, gun ready. Aiming at a bandit galloping toward them at full speed, she cocked the rifle and squinted one eye. A strong arm tugged her sideways before she could pull the trigger, sending her weapon flying from her hands as she fell. A bullet whizzed past them, ricocheting off a rock.

"You're insane." Jack berated her as he pulled her to safety, his hands grazing over her shoulders, arms, and waist. She wasn't sure if he was checking for injuries or just relieved she was alive.

"And you aren't?" Her eyes flashed.

"You should've stayed in the wagon."

"Why didn't you wake me?"

"Now isn't the best time to argue." Reaching across her middle, he grabbed the barrel of her fallen gun and dragged it toward her.

"I'm not trying to argue. How many ways do I have to say it? You'll get yourself killed if you refuse to rely on others."

"Okay, okay. You're right," he said, shrugging. "Take this, you'll need it."

"We need to go back." She looked around, searching for an escape, before accepting the rifle.

"There's a reason we're out here. Do you want stray bullets breaking the wagons, or worse breaking the bodies of our women and children?" Jack reasoned with her and then peeked around the rock. Another bullet cracked against the granite, sending debris flying into the air.

"Of course not," she replied, her voice shaking.

While trying to collect herself, a quick movement caught her eye. Amelia turned in time to see a boot flying toward her hands. The swift kick knocked her gun away and the aggressor stood towering over them, having approached from behind.

Kneeling to raise the gun to Jack's temple, he forced him to put his gun down or face a hole in the head. Amelia began to shake at the prospect of seeing the man she'd grown to care for killed before her eyes. Two days in a row she'd had to witness someone putting a gun to his head. The outlaw was tall and lean with a scar stretching across his right eye and knotted black hair tied at the base of his neck. He reeked of sweat and tobacco.

"Next time I find you, only one of us will walk away," he said, staring down at Jack. "I told you that years ago, and I'm here to keep my promise."

"You," her husband replied with a dangerous edge to his voice.

"Or maybe I should amend my plan and shoot this lady of yours instead." He tipped the gun in her direction then recentered it on Jack.

"Your grievance is with me and no one else."

"Is that any way to talk to your old pal? We were of the same blood once." The bandit cleared his throat and spit on the ground between them. She shuddered.

A Journey for Amelia

"We're nothing alike. I was a confused boy, taking my anger out in all the wrong ways." Jack said, a forlorn look gracing his features.

"You swore your allegiance to me and my men. And then you ran away like a yellow-bellied good for nothing."

"I chose a different path. I knew you'd never agree, so I left."

"In the dead of night, without so much as a word." The man dug his revolver harder into Jack's skin.

Amelia watched the two men, her heart jumping in her chest. Jack had a past, but she'd never imagined it would catch up with them on their journey for a second time. She also knew that he was a skilled fighter, but the man in front of them seemed equally dangerous.

"Please, we don't want any trouble," she said, her voice trembling.

The bandit leader turned to her, his eyes dark and glinting. "Oh, I think we do," he said, a wicked grin spreading across his face. He turned to speak to Jack again. "You see, we've been on your tail for a while now, and I've had my eye on your pretty little woman here for some time."

A wave of nausea washed over Amelia. She'd heard tales of outlaws who took what they wanted but never thought it'd happen to her. The sensation of heavy stones filled her stomach.

"Let her go," Jack said in a hard tone, his brows narrowing. "This is between you and me."

The bandit laughed, a harsh, cruel sound. "Oh, I don't think so. You see, I have a score to settle with you, my old friend. And what better way to do it than by taking what you hold most dear?"

Amelia's mouth gaped as the bandit moved his gun from Jack's head to her chest. Cold metal pressed against her collarbone, and she knew that one wrong move could mean the end of her life. But perhaps that would be more merciful than whatever the bandit leader had in mind.

A solitary tear slipped down her cheek, but she blinked it away. Her mouth closed tight, and she tipped her chin up. She refused to let such a repugnant man make her cry. On the inside, she wished to weep. To wail in fear. But she sat with her head held high.

"A lot of fight in this one," he said, staring down at her with a crazed grin. "Get up."

The desire to refuse rose deep in her chest, but one glance at Jack's expression told her she'd better obey the command. He didn't want her to take any chances. With a heavy sigh, she pushed herself up onto her feet and stared at the man holding the gun to her sternum.

The outlaw reached forward and grabbed her wrist, dragging her to stand next to him. She cried out as he wrapped his free arm around her and held her in front of his body as he peered over her shoulder.

Pointing his gun at Jack again, he cocked it and placed his finger more firmly on the trigger. "Any last words, Jack Doyle?"

As soon as those words left his mouth, Amelia's knees swayed, and her sight blurred. The chaos around her blended into white noise and her blood pulsed in her ears. No, no…she couldn't watch Jack die. Any movement

A Journey for Amelia

from her could set the shot off, but she had no choice but to take a chance.

Eyes lined with tears, she glanced down at Jack. Their vision locked for a moment and with an understanding between them, she swung her elbow as hard as she could, back into the bandit's gut.

The man stumbled, releasing her to clutch his stomach as he groaned. Recovering quicker than she anticipated, he turned and slapped the back of his hand across her face. She gasped and covered her swollen, bleeding lip with her hand and fell to the ground from the impact.

That moment was enough for Jack as he picked up where she left off, taking advantage of the distraction. He knocked the colt .45 out of the outlaw's hand and tackled him, sending both men sprawling on the ground next to her.

Amelia crawled backward, away from the two men, fear coursing through her veins. Jack and the bandit leader rolled around on the ground, exchanging blows and grunts of pain. It was a vicious fight, with neither man showing any sign of backing down.

She wanted to help but knew that she couldn't risk getting in the way. The grunts and growls of the bandit leader grew louder as he tried to overpower Jack, but Jack held his own against the larger man.

The outlaw managed to push Jack off him, and he scrambled for a knife strapped to his belt. Amelia's body jolted as he lunged at Jack with the blade, but he was quick to dodge out of the way. He grabbed the man's wrist, twisting it until he dropped the weapon, and then delivered a powerful punch to his face.

However, the bandit wasn't ready to give up. He twisted down to the ground to grab the knife and swung it up, stabbing it into Jack's side. Amelia screamed as her husband fell to the ground, writhing. Blood poured from the wound, staining the ground crimson.

The outlaw crouched above Jack, a twisted grin on his face. "It ends here" he spat, pulling the knife from his flesh. His victim coughed and sputtered as he raised the knife high once more, ready to plunge it into his heart.

"No! Please!" She screamed, her throat constricting as she shrieked, begged, and cried for mercy. It'd all happened so fast.

In a second, Jack reached out and grabbed the gun that had fallen to the ground. He pointed it at the outlaw and pulled the trigger, sending a bullet straight through the man's chest. The outlaw fell lifeless beside him.

Frozen with shock, it took a few moments for her stiff muscles to thaw. She couldn't believe they were both alive. They'd made it. Nothing could stop the floodgate that opened and released tears to stream down her cheeks. Crawling over to Jack, she wrapped her arms around him the best she could, avoiding his injured side.

He held her tight, his breathing ragged and his grip on her trembling. "It's over now."

"You're hurt," she replied, lifting her body to inspect his side. "We need to stop the bleeding."

She attempted to tear part of her dress to help his wound, but the fabric refused to budge. Her hands flew

A Journey for Amelia

about, and her breathing grew heavy. There was too little time. Focus, she had to focus.

Crawling over to the bandit's corpse, she pried the knife from his hand and cut as much fabric from her underskirt as she could before making her way back to Jack. Gathering the white linen, she pressed it against his side with a firm push.

A strong pair of hands folded over hers, calming her frantic emotions.

"Look at me," Jack said, his tone gentle but firm.

Their eyes met and a warmth spread through her body, reaching deep into her soul.

"Don't leave me," she said with a whimper. "I need you."

"I'll never leave the people I love again. It's a promise." His voice deepened as he drew himself up to prop his back against the rock.

She blinked. Did he mean it? Wait…"Love?"

He nodded, then drew her into his arms. She frowned as he winced.

"But your wound."

"Amelia Wright. I need you to listen." Letting his fingers flow through strands of her hair, he cupped her cheek gently with the other hand. "Whether I have fifty seconds left or fifty years, I will love you for every one of them. Until my very last breath."

"Oh Jack, I love you too," she cried, closing her eyes, and leaning into his touch.

"S'pose I should've courted you first, but here we are. In love and already married," he said, letting loose a laugh that ended in a coughing fit.

"Don't laugh. You'll lose too much blood. Besides," she said, her tone relaxing a fraction. "What would you call all those days on the trail? You've been courting me for months, Jack."

He smirked. "I best take responsibility then."

"Best you do," she replied.

Despite his injury and the chaos surrounding them, he reached a hand behind her head and pulled her down to meet him. His warm breath tinged over her lips and a scent of spice filled her nostrils as their noses touched. Gooseflesh rose over her body and a heat from within filled her from head to toe.

Her eyelashes fluttered, and she held her breath until she realized he was waiting on her to close the rest of the gap—giving her a chance to refuse. Without allowing herself time to second guess, she met him the rest of the way, pressing her lips against his.

The action ignited his movements as he pulled her closer, his hands roaming from her hair to her jawline. His thumb caressed her skin in gentle circles as he deepened the kiss. She sighed against his mouth as they broke for air, his skin soft and his touch gentle.

As she pulled back, her hand slipped from his wound. Berating herself for losing focus, she pushed it back down. When Jack didn't even mutter a single grunt or groan, her eyes snapped to his face. His eyelids were closed, and his breath grew weak.

"Jack!" Panic ripped through her, suffocating her with the thought of losing the man she loved. "Wake up!"

A Journey for Amelia

She shook him softly but still he lay still. He couldn't be gone. Not after everything they'd been through. Desperate to save his life, and her voice cracking from screaming for help, she did the only thing she could. Amelia prayed.

epilogue

AMELIA

Oregon City, Oregon 1867
2 months later

"Well," Thomas cleared his throat then took another sip of coffee. "That's quite an adventure you've had, little sister."

"You could say that," Amelia replied from across the table as she finished recounting their journey.

"I'd ask if Jack survived, but that's rather pointless given the circumstances," her brother said.

"She's the best nurse anyone could hope for," Jack replied with a grin then squeezed his wife's hand. They sat side by side, enjoying the company of her long-sought-after kin in his cozy homestead.

"The rest of the outlaws scattered after they lost their leader. Amelia was bound and determined to keep me alive."

"Sounds like her," Thomas replied with a hearty chuckle.

"The most determined woman I've ever met."

"You're just as strong-willed, mister," she said, pushing her chair back to retrieve the freshly baked pie from the kitchen.

"Better watch yourself," Thomas joked from behind a hand to hide his smile.

"I stand by what I told my wife the day I met her. We'll never have a dull moment in our marriage."

Slicing three pieces of apple pie, she slid them onto plates and then gathered two into her hands. Returning to the table, she placed one in front of her brother and the other in front of herself then sat down. She took a bite and peeked at her husband from the corner of her eye with a mischievous grin.

"I'm not sure why you're taste-testing my slice, but I appreciate it, my love," Jack said as he slid the pie out from beneath her fork and snatched the silverware from her hand.

"Mmm," She mumbled in protest, her mouth still full. He never let her get away with her pranks. Teasingly, she swatted his arm and then stood to retrieve the missing piece so they could all enjoy dessert together.

"Come to think of it, I still owe you that second half payment for putting up with my sister for life."

Jack got a good chuckle out of that. Too good. She rolled her eyes.

"He's right! I should be paid for my services."

"Put the money toward our wedding, Thomas," she chided, purposefully ignoring his attempt to tease her.

Laughter and joy filled Amelia as she visited with the two most important men in her life. When she'd left Missouri, she never imagined the end of her journey would've led her to a full life with Jack, but she wouldn't trade it for the world. In a few weeks they'd have their official wedding ceremony with her brother to walk her down the aisle.

She still missed her parents, but over time she learned that grief could either halt your life or become a part of it. Every step merged to create her personal journey, and she wouldn't take a moment of it back.

And what a terrible but beautiful journey it had been.

The End

This is the second book in the Reluctant Wagon Train Bride series – each book stands alone. To read more, check out the rest of the series:

https://www.amazon.com/dp/B0CDLG11HY

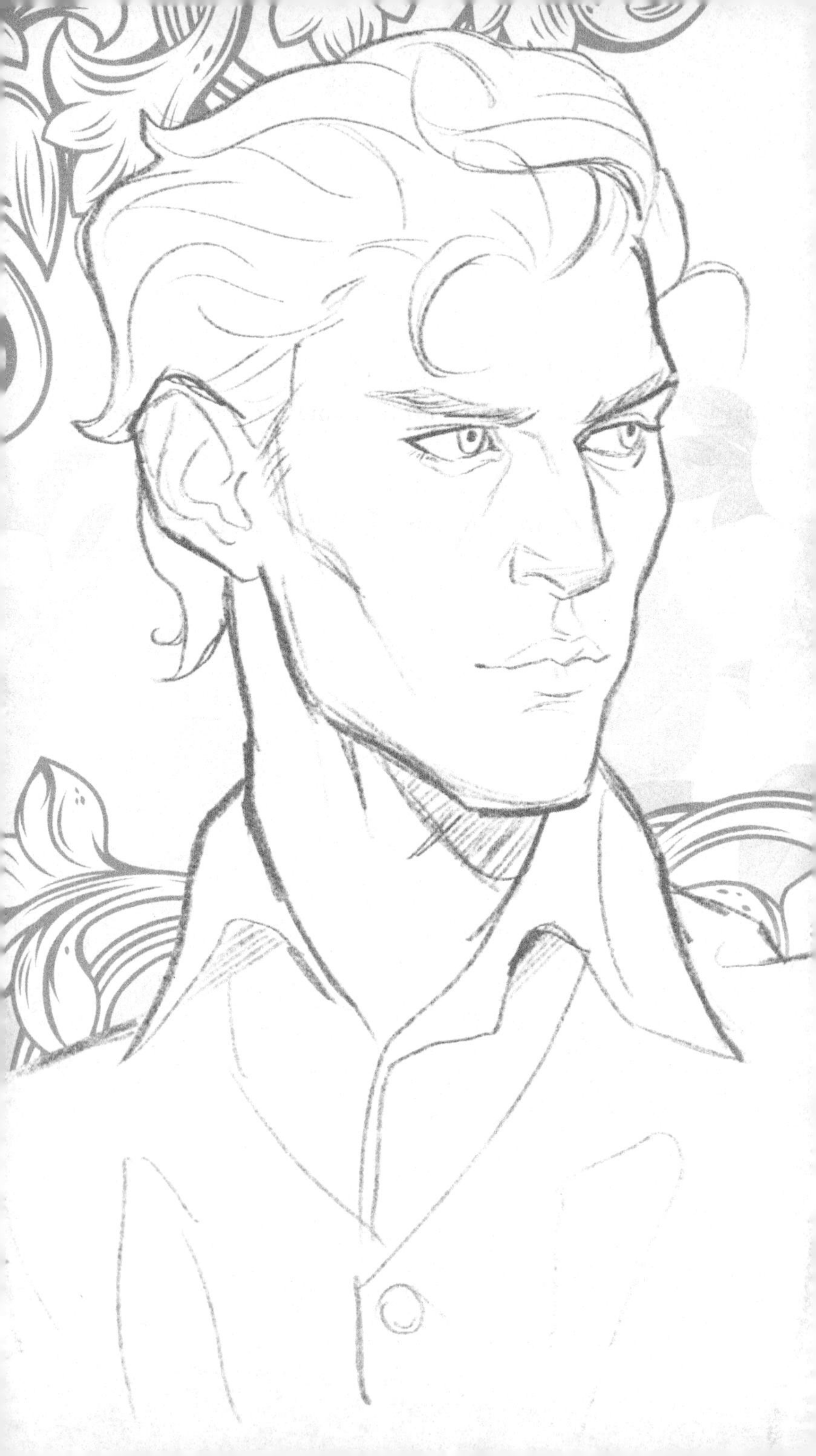

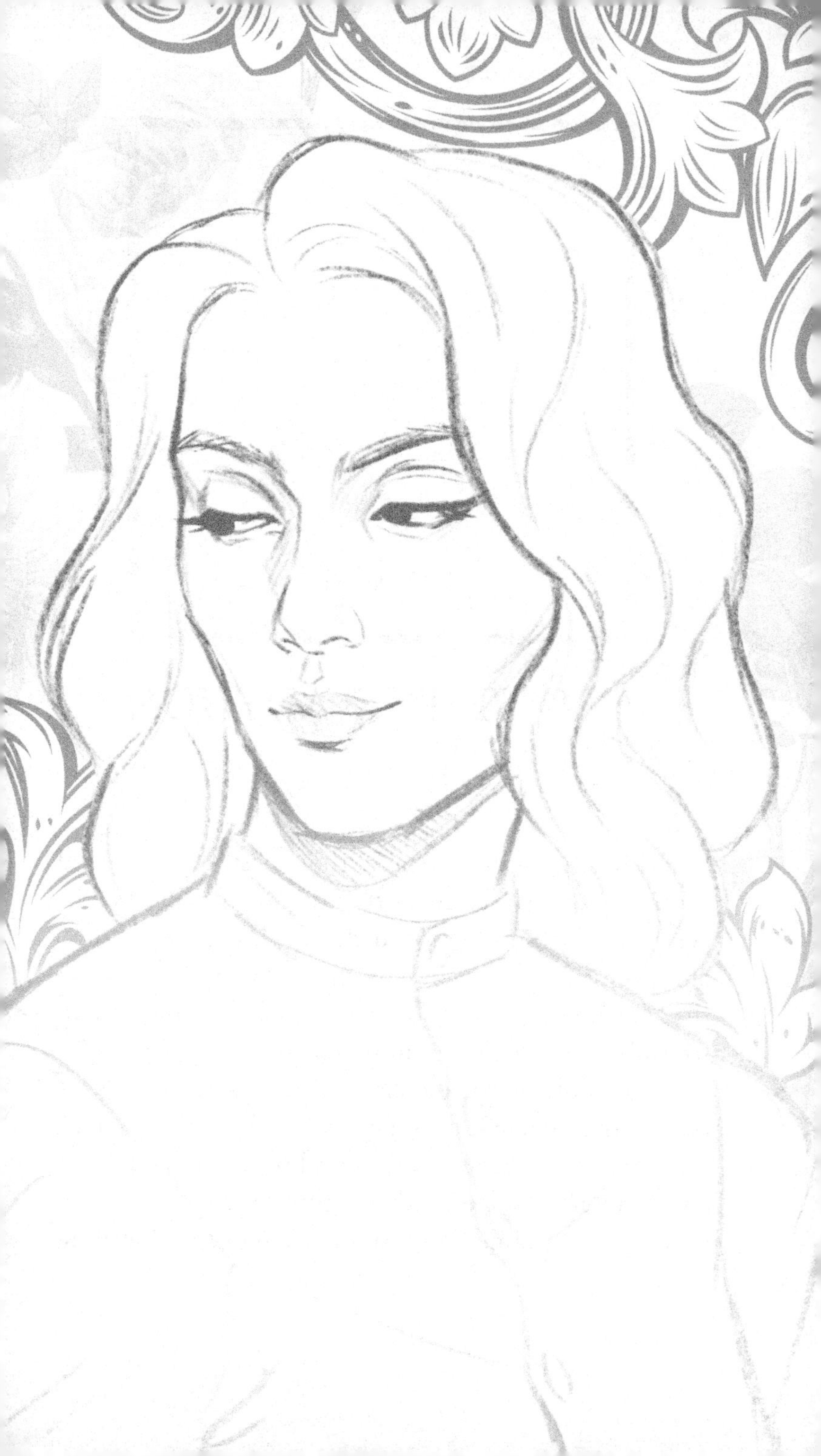

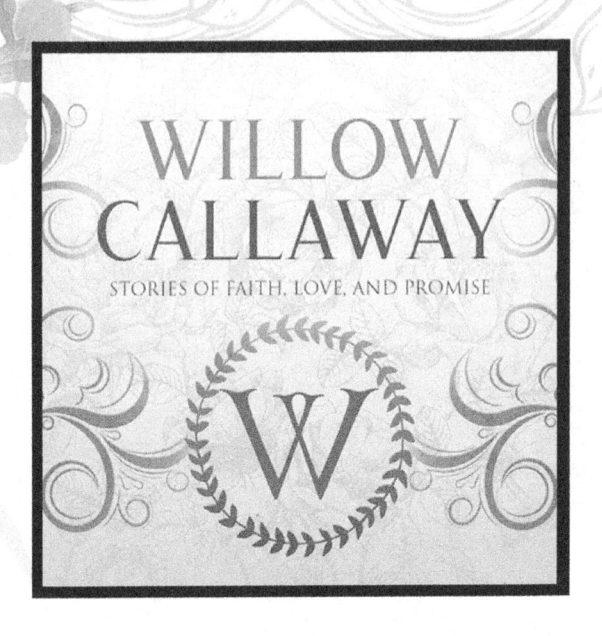

ABOUT THE AUTHOR

Willow Callaway is the author of sweet, historical romance stories. She loves to write about flawed characters who fight for a second chance through faith, love, and promise. Willow lives with her loving husband in the Midwest US where she enjoys reading, painting, and whipping up new recipes in the kitchen.

Living outside the big city has always been her way, but her true dream is to someday move into a cozy country home with a beautiful view and plenty of wild, fresh air. Despite having no children to call her own, she is very close with her family and values them deeply. Nothing brings her more joy than to pour out her imagination through the written word and share it with anyone who stumbles upon her books hoping for a tale that will brighten their mood and lighten their heart.

If you enjoyed this story by Willow, follow her on Amazon and sign up to her newsletter to get the latest on updates, giveaways, and more! Never miss a new release.

https://willowcallaway.com/home#Newsletter

Thank you for reading A Journey for Amelia! Lastly, if you wish to help Willow find further success (and therefore be able to write more often), please feel free to leave a review for her book on Amazon, post about it on social media, or tell a friend! Word of mouth is everything for authors, and they are forever grateful.

Find me online:

Amazon
https://www.amazon.com/stores/author/B0CBP4TFMR/allbooks

Facebook
https://www.facebook.com/willowcallawaybooks

Website
https://willowcallaway.com/

MORE WESTERN ROMANCE

Can't get enough historical romance? If you'd like to discover more stories by Willow Callaway, and her fellow authors P. Creeden and Penny Kate, you can join the My Beta and ARC Reader Group on Facebook!

https://www.facebook.com/groups/363425004581926

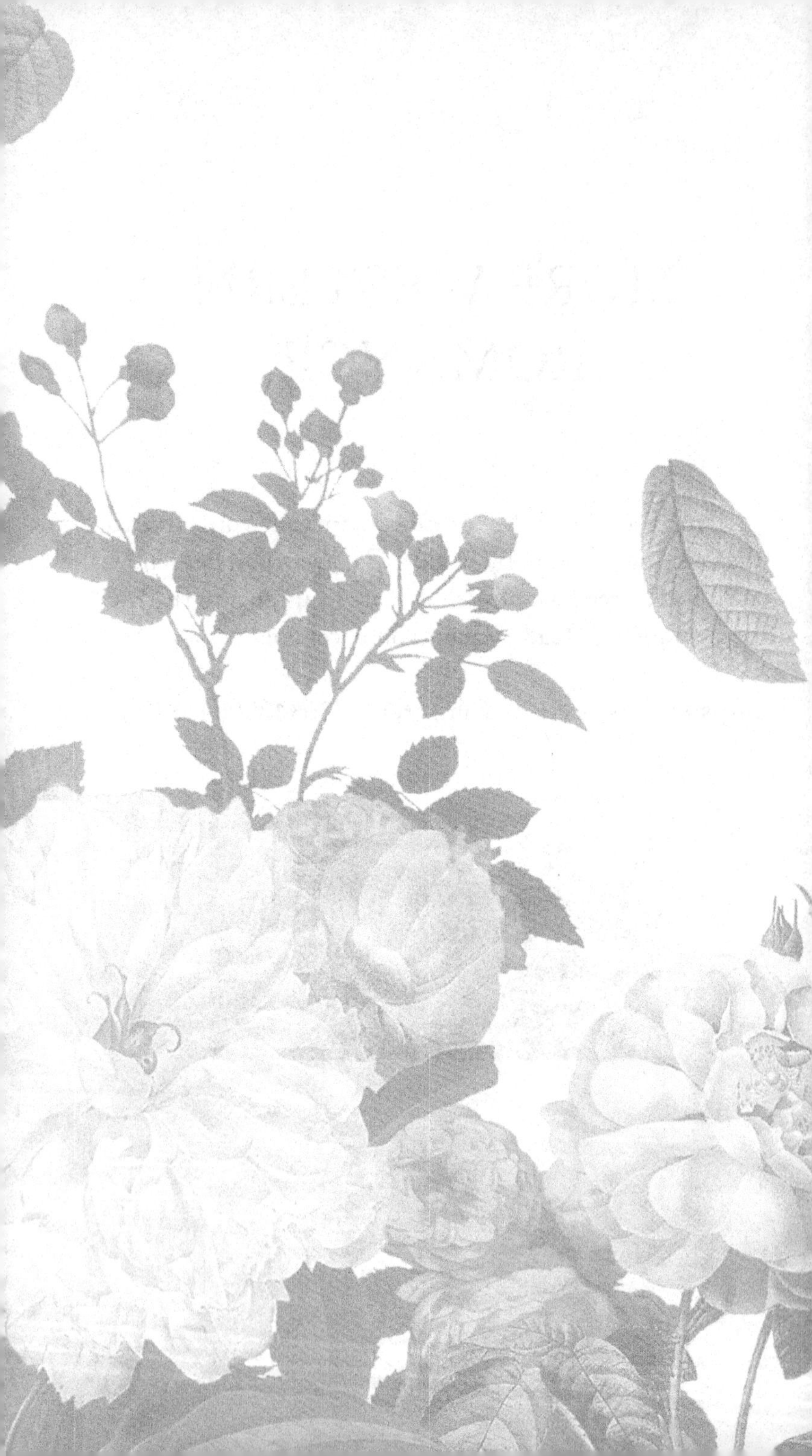

OTHER BOOKS BY WILLOW CALLAWAY

THE MARSHAL'S MAIL-ORDER BRIDE

GRACE'S
Christmas Escape

WILLOW CALLAWAY

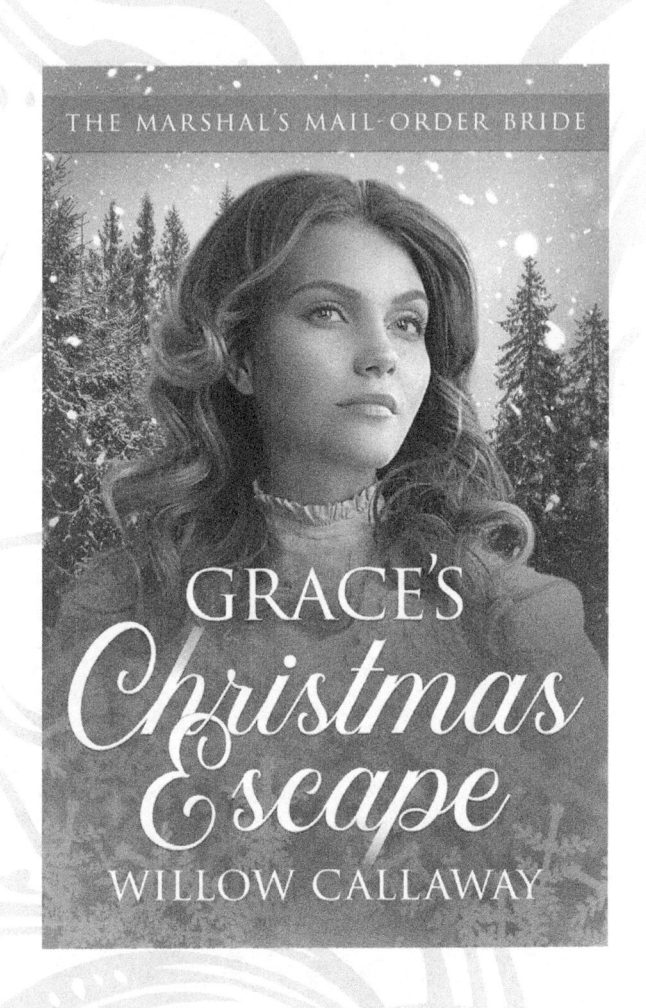

https://www.amazon.com/Graces-Christmas-Escape-Marshals-Order-ebook/dp/B0CDGPW296

GRACE'S CHRISTMAS ESCAPE

A desperate woman ready for a fresh start. A Marshal who refuses to marry. And the arrangement that brings a runaway bride and a reluctant lawman together.

Grace had always dreamed of her wedding day. She'd planned out her perfect life with the perfect fiancé. Or so she'd thought…until the man turns out to be one of the country's most-wanted bank robbers. Now she's on the run too, heading for a small town to meet a man in need of a mail-order bride.

Marshal Wesley refuses to take a wife, no matter how much his mother begs him to settle down. The law is his life, so when he discovers she's ordered him a mail-order bride behind his back he's nothing short of furious. A beautiful blonde with sad eyes shows up on his doorstep claiming to be his bride. Even though he won't wed her, the least he can do is let her stay until she gets back on her feet.

Their match isn't made in heaven, but something draws them together like a moth to the flame. Will they be able to find love in each other, or will outside meddling and an ever-growing danger drive them apart?

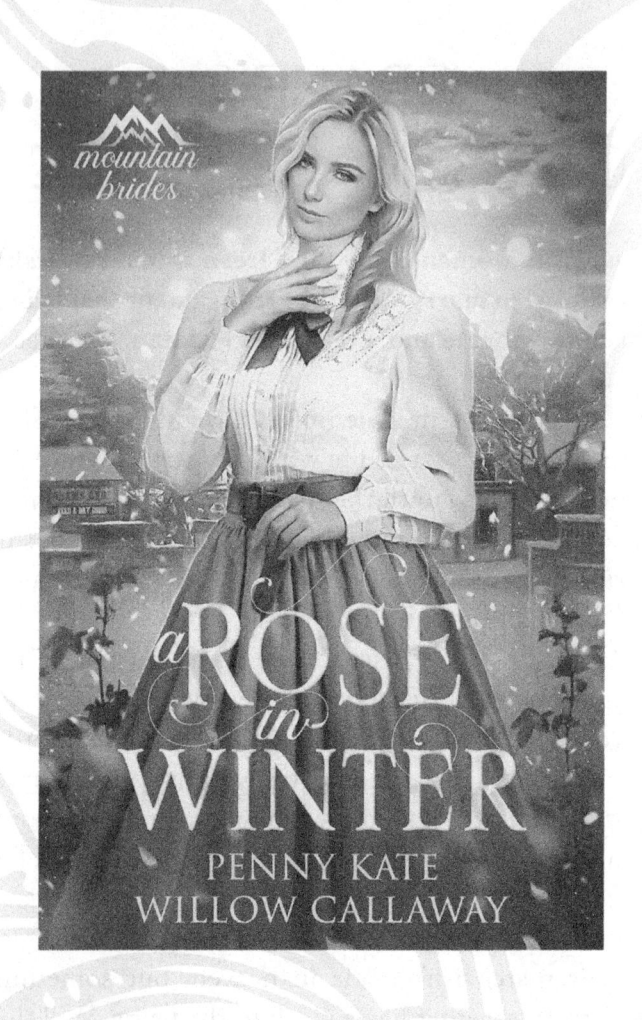

https://www.amazon.com/Rose-Winter-Order-Mountain-Brides-ebook/dp/B0CDML34D1

A ROSE IN WINTER

A mistaken mail-order bride who thinks she's found the perfect match. A reclusive mountain man who swears off matrimony. And an unexpected love that may lead both to a better future.

Arriving in town during a deadly blizzard, Rose is rescued by the man she thinks she's meant to marry, only to find herself stuck with his rough and brooding brother instead. With no clue as to why he's forgotten her, she's fiercely determined to make him remember.

When Warren discovers a lost woman on his mountain who claims they're destined to marry, he's convinced she's lost her senses. Knowing she sustained a head injury, he plays along, but soon the truth unravels to reveal that he's the wrong man, and she's very much the wrong woman.

They'd both rather send her home, but the mountain isn't forgiving, and Rose is forced to stay with him for the rest of an uncomfortable winter. With their lives completely at odds, will misunderstandings drive them apart, or will love find a way?

Made in the USA
Monee, IL
19 May 2024